D1707793

# SHALOM TOWER
# SYNDROME

# SHALOM TOWER SYNDROME

*a novel*

Albert Russo

Library of Congress Control Number:    2007905087
ISBN:            Hardcover            978-1-4257-7726-5
                 Softcover            978-1-4257-7703-6

This book was printed in the United States of America.

**To order additional copies of this book, contact:**
Xlibris Corporation
1-888-795-4274
www.Xlibris.com
Orders@Xlibris.com
35826

# Dedication

To Adam Donaldson Powell
a wonderful friend,
an artist and a poet
par excellence

discover the many facets of this Renaissance man:
www.adamdonaldsonpowell.com

# INTRODUCTION
## by David Alexander

There is a type of novel whose aim, as Jonathan Swift wrote of his intention behind Gulliver's Travels, is to "vex the world rather than divert it." If it's an honest and true-hearted novel, then it will inevitably also serve both as a vexatious testament and a diverting read. Such is Albert Russo's *Shalom Tower Syndrome*.

It may be rare to begin an exploration of a book with its title, except here the title seems to have links to a wide miscellany of things, and a certain way of walking up the walls of the mind and capering on the roof. The Shalom Tower, "Peace Tower," called Migdal Shalom in Hebrew, is a rectangular black monolith that rises at the north end of Herzl Street in Tel Aviv. It overlooks the main city of a nation to whom peace has always seemed like the eye of a hurricane, and whose capital, Jerusalem, has a reputation of working strange thaumaturgy on the mind and soul. So the title functions as a neurosemantic shuttlecock. Linguistic interconnections are constantly caroming off the skull's interior.

The first meanings that spring to mind for the phoneme of "syn" in "syndrome" have sexual connotations; original sin, sin in the Garden of Eden; the act of conception, thus the fuck itself, as arch and primeval evildoing. And yet the dictionary rewards one's lexicographical sleuthing with a surprise: the first definitions cited for the noun are religious! Sin means, first and foremost, estrangement from God, secondly, an act regarded by theologians as a transgression of God's will. And then another surprise— not only is sin also the 21st letter of the Hebrew alphabet, it is the name for the Mesopotamian god of the moon, the counterpart of the Sumerian Nanna.

The Encyclopedia of Gods on my reference shelf relates that Sin, whose consort is Nikkal, (she who bore the sun god Utu) is symbolized by the new moon and perceived as a bull whose horns are the crescent of the moon. I now ponder the significance of "horns" as they relate to Russo's novel, which is replete with the lunar messages of sex as from time to time grace our dreams with manic copulations, and especially the significance of the obscene gesture, known throughout Italy as *Il Cornuto*, which calls those to whom it is aimed cuckolds, men who have lost control of their women, thus their manhood, and thus, in this Mediterranean culture still steeped in ancient madnesses, their lives. For in *Shalom Tower Syndrome*, the protagonist, Alexis, born in Africa to a mother who was a *metisse*, or a woman of mixed bloodlines, and to a father who was a Jew, has arrived at a point in which both his life and his marriage have come undone and where Alexis' consciousness has dissolved into what psychologists call a fugue state in which past, present and future seem to merge, or more appropriately, collide.

"You feel something leaking in you but don't known where it originates," relates Alexis early on by way of explaining the reasons why he and his wife Serena chose to "break from our grim, smog-filled Milan environment" and commence a series of peregrinations to the antipodes of the globe and the soul. "You even cease to be aware of it. Because for a while the leaking abates. Then a drought settles in, sweeping through your plexus, and at this state the process becomes irreversible. The walls inside you begin to crack . . . ."

In literary terms such a fugue state could be further classified as a coex system, a term coined by psychologist Stanislaus Grof to describe the state marked by dissolved psychic boundaries such as those made manifest in James Joyce's novels, like Ulysses; a state which, according to Grof, bears marked resemblances to the fugue state experienced under the influence of LSD and other psychedelic drugs as well as to the trauma of birth.

At any rate, perhaps because "whom the gods would destroy they first make mad," the next word that freely associates after *cornuto* is the Italian, "pazzo," crazy, a word that connotes, at least to the Mafia, who call those afflicted with it "potts" or "potsy," the pretext for a hit on one who has lost the respect of his peers. Curious that the book's protagonist, Alexis, is going slowly crazy in Jerusalem, that he embodies a chain of causality between estrangement from God, sexual transgression, and the cuckolded husband. And, something else—I mentioned before that sin is also the 21st letter of the Hebrew Alphabet, add the numerals together, as do the sages of the Kabala, and you get—three. Curioser and curioser: Russo's narrative begins to take shape, from the very first lines of chapter two, with a dissertation on the significance of the triad in Alexis' life:

> Triality . . . Tri . . . Three . . . Trial . . . Trial of a lifetime. The full word epitomizing the existential qualm for which my heritage is responsible: Africa, Judaism and Italy. They clash and coexist in cycles, in a fashion so inchoate that I am never quite sure which will take the upper hand.

Running through this voyage through the fugue states of a coex system is the concept of the Trinity, whose multiple associations with religion, sexual ménages à trois, multiple personalities, multiple personal and national origins, snake through the warp and woof of the storyline and are visible at nearly every point in it.

And then there is also the phoneme "drome." Aerodrome, Videodrome Signals, arenas, amphitheaters, Roman Colosseums are evoked. Here a consultation with Webster's yields fresh conundrums, for a drome is defined as an airfield equipped with, among other things, a control tower. A tower! Yes, a sin drome. A tower of sin, a Triune sin, that is also a trial for this pilgrim to Jerusalem, whose name means City of Peace. And was it not high towers on whose exposed summits Syrian pillar hermits—the "stylitoe" who modeled their peculiar self-mortifications after the first of their number, Simeon Stylites—squatted to endure the privations of the desert in order to cleanse their souls of sin?

Somehow, as I write this, I hear the voice of a patch of cells in the language center of my brain I call The German, saying "schau das an," which in the Austrian dialect of German whose early inundation of the formative ego by a family still residing mentally in Europe doubtless conceived the seed-germ of that dab of nerve tissue means "look at this." Why should I be thinking "look at this" in childhood German as I ponder the neurosemantic, Joycean fugue aspects of the title? I try to run this down: Shalom also sounds to me like Salome, a possible variation on the Hebrew word for Peace, and also the name of a treacherous harlot who, in dancing lasciviously before the biblical King Herod, secured the beheading of John the Baptist.

Am I to "look" in "drome," and the hidden sinews that form the connective tissue binding together the phallic architecture from whose vantage point one can "look out" over Tel Aviv with the best view of the city and the insights the book offers into the psychopathology of sexual power politics, that leads to the tantalizing thought that the book is a "drome," i.e., a field or amphitheater of barbaric divertissements topped by a Mephistophelian column from whose heights one can have a view into the Heart of Darkness below (another title, by the way, of a book that like this one concerns Africa), and by so doing attempt to cleanse one's soul?

And what of Alexis, the name of the book's antihero? The name rings no bells in the mental belfry, but Alexius does: Alexius I Comnenus, the 11th Century Byzantine emperor, inspired the First Crusade. Jerusalem again. City of Peace, as we've pointed out. And also, city of a peculiar sin drome, or syndrome, based on a usually temporary religio-maniacal psychosis known clinically as Jerusalem Syndrome. And it is for sure that the character of Alexis has developed this mental dysfunction from practically the first moment of his arrival in Jerusalem.

Not quite, though, for like the vast majority of those diagnosed with Jerusalem Syndrome, Alexis has already gone crazy. We suspect early on, then become increasingly aware, that Alexis has come to Jerusalem to die, perhaps even to rise reborn, like another who once came riding into the city on an ass to be crucified at around the same time of year—Israel Independence Day—that the narrative's time frame encompasses. And, indeed, the obsession with a goal or mission of grandiose, even Apocalyptic, import that takes hold of the afflicted, may sometimes result in attempts to end their peculiar sufferings by enduring a Christlike death, often in a "high place," which, in the absence of a handy Golgotha, the Place of the Skull in Old Aramaic (also called Calvary, and believed to lie on the site on which the Church of the Holy Sepulchre was built), may well present the aspect of a Tower of Peace:

> I walk away from him, brush past several other tourists and locate a narrow space entrenched between two metallic columns. It is small but wide enough for a person of my build to climb over the guardrail and wedge himself sideways in it. I make sure no one comes near me, at least during the few seconds I need in order to hurl myself into the void. With a little effort, I am able to reach the guardrail, but as I am about to climb over it, the left side of my shorts gets hooked onto a sharp edge. Rage mixed with a

growing sense of panic takes hold of me, and the more I try to wrench myself out of the nail-like object, the fiercer my shorts cling to it, in spite of its widening tear.

A woman's voice suddenly booms out: "Somebody, quick! There's a guy who wants to jump off."

Alexis' suicide attempt ends in a seriocomic burlesque of tragedy. But the bizarre chain of events that has afflicted him since his arrival in Israel, that has caused him to quit his wife in Jerusalem for a junket to Tel Aviv with a complete stranger, and that has knocked him into a fugue state of towering dimensions, has also brought him face to face with hidden currents of his being that afflict his mind as the most unimaginable of mortal sins. Arrived in Israel the underpinnings of reality have given way beneath his feet. Alexis is a man already toppled from the pinnacle of a psychic tower of peace, that fanciful pedestal constructed from the trappings of the conventional "good" life he'd left behind when he set foot in Israel. He is a man already falling through space on a downward trajectory from sin to drome. Why not make it official and die for real?

Alexis doesn't, and while the event marks a monumental turning point in his life, it's not the sort of plot dénouement that is attended by the trappings of literary melodrama which, as in the real world, as in this novel, seldom reveal their impact on the outer universe though they leave profound imprints on the inner streams of being. Just as it is in some ways reminiscent of Joyce's *Ulysses*, *Shalom Tower Syndrome* shares attributes with Eric Ambler's tales of "innocents abroad," but it also shares a great deal with those 19th and early 20th century authors of the *roman à clef*, "romances with a key," especially those penetratingly insightful books and stories written by the Swiss novelist Hermann Hesse that Hesse dubbed *Seelenbiographie* or "biographies of the soul." *Shalom Tower Syndrome* is very much a modern biography of the soul, and onto its pages Russo seems to have poured out dark secrets and lustrous truths dredged from the depths of his being.

Fiction writer and poet of great talent, *David Alexander* is also well-known for his literary essays and his technothrillers, for which Richmond Observer calls him "the king of action-adventure writing". Right now, he says he is physically in New York but mentally in Rome.

Look up his website: http://davidalexanderbooks.com/

# CHAPTER ONE

Bloodcurdling scenes. Emaciated faces blown up on the circular wall. Expressions in shades of gray. My head begins to spin. I feel numb, mentally numb. This is a museum, isn't it? I hear the syncopated sighs of an elderly woman. Not far from her a little boy stares at his mother: she's weeping. Do people weep in museums? He seems puzzled, but he senses the gravity surrounding him and knows better than to ask questions. Everyone here looks so gloomy, so somber. Even the fat lady over there, wearing that ridiculous hat in the shape of a bird's nest. Such young children shouldn't be dragged to places like this. There will be enough occasions for them to suffer. Suffer . . . what does it mean? All of a sudden I feel a tightness inside of me. The pain . . . in my chest. I'm gasping for air. Serena has noticed and whispers: "Don't stay here. Go to the garden. I'll join you in a moment."

The sun is a reddish-yellow color, like the yolk of a monstrous egg, smouldering and about to explode over the desert. I shield my eyes against its glare. A soothing sound seeps into my brain. It is the putt putt of a sprinkler. Smell of newly mown grass.

At the far end of the kibbutz a cluster of jonquils stands guard before the wreckage of a WWII monoplane. Everything here seems incongruous: the neat, low-roofed bungalows, the futuristic museum whose wooden panels make it look like a church designed by Le Corbusier. The orange grove that stretches eastward of a mock battlefield with its war paraphernalia: trenches, rolling hills, ambushed trucks, wounded soldiers, the young boy holding a grenade behind an overturned tank, and a little further, covering two bodies, the remnants of a white and blue flag with the Star of David.

Gazing at the horizon, I perceive another soldier mannikin whose body lies stretched on the ground, his left arm thrust above his head and holding a handkerchief; he must have been waving it in desperation. Devilish reconstruction of yesterday's and possibly tomorrow's gruesome reality. Twittering of birds. Children giggling near me. I can almost hear them breathing. Like those flowers burgeoning over the gangrenous crust of earth. Defiance of adversity. Some call it arrogance.

Serena comes out of the museum, chatting with a bearded, silver-haired man. Striking features. Obstinate forehead. He could be handsome. An Akademaim? Maybe. She has a flair for the uncommon, the eccentric, and the peculiar. And very often I agree with her choice. But now, I can't be bothered.

"Alec, this is Mr. Kishon who's a researcher at the Weizmann Institute."

"Your wife tells me that you are staying in Ashkelon. I spend my weekends there."

He rolls his r's in that distinct Sabra manner which is at once virile and a trifle insolent. It has its charm, sometimes, depending on who uses it. I really don't want to start a conversation. Let her do the talking. I'm getting a headache, I think.

"Serena, Mr . . . er . . ." I utter.

"Kishon, Dave Kishon."

"Yes, well, please excuse me, I'm feeling nauseous again." And it's no lie either.

During our ride back on the sherut—a marvellous meeting place, those collective taxis—I entrench myself behind the screen of tightly closed lids. Not a comfortable position, I admit, but it's the only deterrent against verbal assault.

A couple and a woman whom I greeted when I got in the cab are babbling away in Hebrew. I grasp a word here and there, especially when it is the person with the singsong who talks. Are they discussing family matters, work? The man has coarse fingers and a rugged skin. He laughs heartily, digging a nudge into my ribs. To excuse himself, he growls an endless 'sorrrry', shakes my hand until I can hear the knuckles grit.

"Oh, that's okay!"

I could bash his head, but keep smiling instead—eyes shut again to discourage any familiarity. I lend an ear to the other side. Serena's arm rubs against mine each time the car jolts over a bump. She and that physicist are exchanging views.

"Yesterday two patrolmen were booby-trapped on the outskirts of Gaza. I don't advise you to go there, even under escort."

What did he say his name was again? Kishon! Would he be related to Efraim Kishon, the satirist? I like his wit. By the way, I forgot to buy the weekend issue of the Jerusalem Post. That's when they feature his stories. Strange that I should have discovered him in Germany, of all places. He's so often on the bestseller list there. In Italy nobody's heard of him.

First stop. Out you go, the three of you. Chatterboxes!

"Shalom shalom. Enjoy your stay."

I've lost the notion of laughter, let alone of enjoying things. Who ever gave me the idea of coming here, in my state? Land of milk, honey and blood. Land of exacerbation, where the value of each human being is so high and . . . volatile, that considering one's ailments becomes almost ludicrous.

Never has the Jewish 'third' of me suffered from such acute estrangement while at once tightening its grip on my anima. Insidious, undaunted, it creeps under my skin as if to take revenge against the disregard I have so far shown toward its atavistic presence. I feel it stinging every one of my pores, clipping the raw ends of my fibers. In turn sweet and so acrid. A quagmire in which I am slowly drowning as the other two elements of my existential stuff dissolve. Whose blood is heavier to bear? That of Astrid, my beautiful mulatto mother converted to Catholicism by a missionary in Congo/Zaire? Or that of her husband who considered himself Florentine above all and peripherally, yes only peripherally Jewish? Whom should I hold responsible for the twelve years of Christian education I was exposed to while we lived in the Belgian Congo? Too long the Jewishness in me has been latent, neglected, taken for granted, like the myriad of antibodies which automatically build up in one's organism.

"This is it!" Serena tells the sherut driver, handing him a ten pound note.

"I'll get off too," decides Mr. Kishon, "my house is just a few blocks away."

As he walks us to the porch of our pension he turns to me and uses an unexpectedly soft tone:

"How's that headache of yours? Won't you join me this evening for dinner? I'll make some barbecued lamb."

I stare at him then stare at Serena, not that I'm waiting for her to answer. The concept of time has left me ever since I first set foot in this country.

"I'd be delighted . . . he too, no . . . Alexis?"

Looking through her, I nod an unconvincing 'yes'.

He produces a stained piece of paper from his shirt pocket, draws a map and jots down an address. Which he gives to my wife.

"*Tov*, I'll be expecting you around 8:30. OK?"

Whereupon he takes leave of us.


I hear a rustle from beneath the hedge. Such noises make me shudder. Is it a scorpion, a snake? No, it's that little kitten I saw the other day crossing the backyard. The feline population here is enormous. They're all over the place. Stray cats roaming from house to house, from apartment block to apartment block, from shops to outdoor cafes. There always seems to be a bowl of milk or scraps of food waiting for them somewhere. They're as free as the birds; the people here take their nomadic life for granted and seem totally happy with the situation, for I've never seen cats living indoors, as they do in Europe or in America.

"Kitty, kitty, kitty." I lure it with a play of fingers, then finally lift it. But now the kitten gets hysterical, sticks out its claws and digs them into the lower part of my arm.

"Let go, you pest!" I groan.

It hisses and writhes as if it were the prey. I thrust the animal to the ground with all my might. Hollow thump of a furry mass which rolls over itself before disappearing in the underbrush. Looking at the shredded geography of my flesh, I can almost hear the silky sound of pain. Ha, Cats of the Holy Land!

We're upstairs, in our bedroom. Serena is applying mercurochrome to my wound. She remains silent. I've noticed the wrinkles of lassitude on her face. A slight arching of the eyebrows, more eloquent than any other words. For Serena never gets into a temper. I am the extrovert, the nervous one. I was, at least until it happened several months ago. It started so quietly, so unobtrusively. You feel something leaking in you but don't know where it originates. It's slow and internal. You even cease to be aware of it. Because for a while the leaking abates. Then a drought settles in, sweeping through your plexus, and at this stage the process becomes irreversible. The walls inside begin to crack, like those of a cobnut tree battered by sandstorms. Yet, no one around you seems to hear the whistling of the gusts of wind, nor can they witness its corrosive effects. You're endowed with an extra pair of eyes, eyes which are turned inward, facing a landscape you are discovering for the first time, like that projected on a three-dimensional screen; but with one difference: you're both spectator and protagonist. The ambiguity reaches such proportions that you find yourself trapped between two equally 'real' worlds; and end up walking on the edge of a dam.

It manifested itself last winter. Serena and I decided to take a break from our grim, smog-filled Milan environment. We wished to avoid the Christmas throngs and the merry-go-rounds of vanity that so typify resorts like Cortina D'Ampezzo or Sestrieres. And we ended up in a tiny mountain village named Chiesa in Valmalenco.

During the day we walked through snow-covered fields and climbed the slopes that led to a tumble-down mansion—ideal set for a horror movie. There, we'd part company, for Serena would return to the village on skis. The crispness of the air, the quality of the light, especially at night when the moon seemed so near, brushing the peaks, ready to topple down in a majestic avalanche at the slightest sound, were too much for me to bear. It was as though someone had taken an oath of silence on my behalf.

When I joined Serena in bed on the afternoon of New Year's Day, I fumbled for words, eyed her childishly and waited until she nodded before slipping into the ritual of lovemaking. We swayed in gentle tides, our movements obeying the mysterious commands of each other's impulses—impulses attuned to seven years of empathic chemistry. We climaxed together, mute, like first-time lovers gripped by fear and remorse. I had the sensation that something terribly stale had been wrung from my body, something ominous.

I got tense and felt gloomy, musing over a book I'd brought with me. It recounted the ordeal of two Rumanian sisters who had been released after thirteen years' imprisonment, for alleged anticommunist spying. No previous story had affected me to this extent. Not Solzhenitsyn's *Day in the Life of Ivan Denisovich*, not even the deportation of my own grandparents. The fact that I'd met one of the sisters couldn't in itself explain the landslide in my emotional center of gravity. I acquired a taste, no, a craving for pain. It became so overpowering that even the contemplation of beauty hurt me, as it does now, as if my eyelids were glued together and had to be brutally unsealed.

Serena is getting dressed for tonight's dinner. I have this sudden urge to exhibit my nudity. I want her to fondle me and make me come in her mouth, without my lifting a single finger. But she's busy applying mascara and tilts her head before the mirror with that half-absent look of hers which has always aroused in me—and in others as well—a sense of tenderness mixed with fascination. I often liked to tease her for being an American:

"You're terribly mysterious for a Yankee!"

She'd smile back as if to say: "What do you really know about America?"

Mr. Kishon hands me a plate of humus.

"If you don't mind, I'd rather taste this feta cheese."

"The view from here is absolutely breathtaking," Serena remarks. It's true, one wouldn't expect to see such high cliffs in this area. I walked along the ridge yesterday. It was desolate and quite awesome. I could have tried to jump but lacked the courage. Too dramatic. Sometimes I envy spies, if only for the fact that they can dispose of their lives so . . . discreetly. All it takes is a small dose of cyanide. I can just imagine their grinning masks: "Talk of crass amateurism!"

Serena and our host are busy turning the skewers over a primitive brick hearth. The prurient sputter of the logs and the lamb's virile smell make my mouth water.

Glints of copper weave through Serena's hair. Two hands couldn't cup her mane, it's so thick.

There's a frankness I like about Mr. Kishon—well, Dave. I feel rotten, but not uncomfortable; he gives the impression of seeing further than my white lie about the headache.

"Alec, help yourself to some shish-kebab, before it all disappears. I'm as hungry as a bear."

He chuckles while aligning three skewers on the plate Serena is holding for me.

Is it the breeze, the spicy aroma of grilled meat, this veranda from which the night and the sea blend into a soothing purgatory? Anyway, my nerves aren't so tense. To be enjoying food without gulping it down as if it were the Last Supper is an experience I've almost forgotten. Pleasantness has become indeed very strange to me. A strangely pleasant evening. I don't remember much of it, except that I spoke about my love for the Black Continent, and the seventeen years I spent in Central Africa. Then the shock of Milan, its bustling, industrialized tempo. And my 'triality'.

# CHAPTER TWO

Triality . . . Tri . . . Three . . . Trial . . . Trial of a lifetime. The full word epitomizing the existential qualm for which my heritage is responsible: Africa, Judaism and Italy. They clash and coexist in cycles, in a fashion so inchoate that I am never quite sure which will take the upper hand.

I've been up since one A.M., reread a passage of the book on the two Rumanian sisters—an obsession; tried to prepare an itinerary for next week, but couldn't. I switched the bed lamp on and off a dozen times. In spite of my being a nuisance to myself, I managed to keep Serena quiet, wringing from her a groan of protest now and then. Thank God she sleeps so soundly! Otherwise we'd need twin beds, not to mention another room—as this one is the size of a lion's den.

Serena's head is turned toward the wall. Her hand resting on my pillow twitches. It often does that when she's waking up. I like the fragrance of her body. Is she beautiful? Not really. Attractive, yes. There's a rare quality about her, she's so neat, even now as she lies in bed. It must be the curls in her hair. Those copper threads shimmering at the most trivial of occasions. They have mesmerized me from the moment I first cast my eyes upon them.

It happened at the American Center in Milan. She was sitting with another girl in the projection room, a couple of rows in front of me. After the performance—an almost apologetic documentary about female violence in the U.S.—I followed them to the library where works of art were on display. I wasn't sure how I should approach her, until I overheard her friend whisper: "Oh, oh, here comes Casanova. Leave it to me!"

I didn't give her a chance to open her mouth. I went straight to Serena and addressed her as if we were alone. I could feel the other girl's resentment. I trusted my intuition and knew I wasn't committing a faux pas. As a matter of fact, Serena, who promptly realized the motive of my behavior, seemed to welcome this 'intrusion'.

I learned later on that her companion, the daughter of a Nebraska senator, had been a passing acquaintance, one of those people whose social life revolves around the cliques that form and dissolve so quickly in cultural centers. Adjusting her sunglasses, the Nebraskan girl uttered a lackadaisical comment and left.

Serena, who was staying at the university's *Città degli Studi*, was preparing a thesis on the poet Cesare Pavese.

She had another trimester left before returning to her native Baltimore. This was time enough to divert the course of two life streams and weave that supple line called bondage into the web of destiny. A line which surreptitiously closed itself into the circle where I am now encased. A line in fact that probably never was straight . . . like the mental distortions caused by our inherent short-sightedness . . . like the belief so long held that the earth was flat . . . like . . .

Mrs. Lindner, the owner of the pension, brings us our breakfast herself, downstairs in the dining room. She knows I do not eat in the morning, yet urges me to "have at least two soft-boiled eggs and fresh toasted scones. You can't start the day on an empty stomach. Bad habits, Mr. Alexis, bad habits. I've prepared fried fish and chicken sandwiches for today's picnic."

I'm quite irritable: those erratic sleeping hours, those totally blank nights. If this were a hotel, I'd leave the dining room at once. Old folks are just about the only people I seem to tolerate. So I can't really get angry with her. Sprightly grandma Lindner! Worrying about "how we could get this young man of ours back into shape. Melancholy doesn't suit him. Right, Mrs. Serena?"

I catch a glimpse of my wife. The twitch of her mouth—at the usual corner—, as if in response to my own helplessness. The line of communication has been interrupted between the two of us, sabotaged—a truncated wire lying deep in the ocean bed. Will I ever find out where? The question suddenly becomes unbearable. A harrowing pain wrenches my lungs. They seem made of alabaster, hard and heavy, weighing on the flesh. I turn to the old lady, grasp her arm:

"Can you give me the address of a psychiatrist? I am sick . . . very sick."

The poor woman is nonplussed, her gaze flits from Serena to me, then back to Serena. She stutters, says something to the tune of:

"Let me call my nephew. He . . . he's a doctor at Tel Ashomer." Before she goes any further, I literally flee out of the building, dragging my bathing towel along and shouting in a frenzy:

"Down by the big rock . . . the ruins . . . the cliff . . ."

The last word breaks out into a sob—thunderous; a generating force that lifts me up in mid-air. My legs are so light, ethereal, as though they've ceased to be part of me. I'm carried away by the magic of speed, hardly feeling the lacerating stings which the blackberry bush inflicts upon my ankles. As I continue to scamper through the thorny paths, the exhilaration reaches levels until now unexplored: I can almost see those streams of icy vapor circling in my head, illuminating at once images of my past with the clarity of a lit-up fir tree.

Orgy of memories, some totally disconnected, others so long forgotten that I hardly recognize them.

As though I were more than the repository of a single man's life, I suddenly acquire the feeling—outlandish—of possessing within my own 'weightlessness' something invaluable: the aggregate of humanity's enigmas. Or is it their answers? If so, they are as indecipherable as a tangled reel of microfilm. In this chaos of data, my newly found recollections stand out as the only possible refuge.

Swimming underwater has an exorcising effect on me. Is that where I belong, amidst the inhabitants of primeval ages? Where violence is of a different kind. Where my nudity is taken for granted. Millions of years of frustration. My whole body arches to make love to the sea—an act of androgynous magnitude through which, in spite of ourselves, nature and I blend. Communion of liquid and sperm, water and fluid. Might our narcissistic inclinations be no more than the vain will to self-inseminate? Its unrealizable fulfillment being at the root of so many of our sorrows? No disturbance in this isolated creek, except for that stupid oil barrel clanging against the coral reef.

When will I tell Serena about the letter of resignation? I've dedicated almost a fourth of my life to KBI Italia.

Almost a decade in that place! "A consortium whose field of action covers the globe, from the industrialized markets of the West to countries as varied as Poland and South Africa, Uruguay and Russia."

How did I ever get involved in such trafficking? On the eve of our departure I destroyed all my business cards:

> Alexis Romani
>
> Export Dept.
>
> Representative of KBI Milan

Signor Giordano's praises still ring in my ears: ". . . with Mr. Romani you will be in good hands. He's one of our top-notch young men. In fact . . ."

Yes, Signor Giordano, in me you had indeed caught a trophy. Mea culpa. I shouldn't have enticed you so with my 'versatile capabilities'. You acted as my spiritual godfather until you decided I was ripe to meet with Mr. Bansei in Tokyo. Hiro, as you derisively called him. Hiro after the Emperor . . . or an abbreviation of Hiroshima?

When I returned from my two-week-long initiation trip in Japan things gradually changed between the two of us. You still liked me but couldn't swallow my newly acquired independence. After all, KBI Italia is out of Signor Giordano's jurisdiction; and although it was somewhat expected, you suddenly realized that I no longer could take orders from you—only suggestions or advice.

"I've made you, Alec. You're the son I've never had."

Poor, childless man! You loved to hear yourself talking this way, didn't you? It had an awkward resonance: nostalgia mixed with revenge. Almost like that of a husband who's deliberately pushed his wife into the arms of another man and doesn't know how to claim her back.

"Beware, Alec, one has to be extra cautious with the Japanese mind. It is as unpredictable as a clear pond which turns into a swamp overnight." These were your fears, Sig. Giordano. Fears that I might one fine morning give you the slip, aiming for the 'enviable' position you've been so long identified with. But you've miscalculated, and grossly so. We've rubbed elbows for ten years, yet you still see gold when the color has faded out completely—at least where I am concerned.

Since the departure of my father you've entrusted yourself with the responsibility of my career. A burden much too heavy for your shoulders, Sig. Giordano—an unnecessary one at that! And what little psychology you have! Before sending me off on that initial African tour, you slipped a couple of hundred dollars into the pocket of my jacket:

"This is for the evenings, to release your tensions. There's nothing like a young Negro pussy, I can assure you. But be careful!"

You always seem to forget about my Congolese background, disregarding the fact that my mother is a métisse, a half-caste, that I am not 'pure' white. You don't spare any remarks about the alleged cupidity of the Jews either. Am I not of the type of whom people so readily say, by way of apologizing after a sly remark, or even as a compliment (!): "But you don't look Jewish . . . and certainly not African."

All in all, you are a kindly person, Sig. Giordano. Even kindly folks are entitled to prejudices. It is not you, rather what you represent and have instilled in me that I despise: the notion of a good Samaritan who flirts with the Untouchable Greats of this world—the business intelligentsia, or should we call it . . . embezzlelentsia— a genus above suspicion. You belong to that category. Not I, at least not any more. You see, mine has been an exhausting journey in Revolution, one so quiet that no one, apart from Serena, could foretell my present state of mental collapse. Yet how honest I felt, planning it, trying to operate with tools devised by the existentialists. They obviously proved to be defective.

You never did take any real interest in the quarterly I founded. Pity, for had you followed the issues of these last two years a little more closely, you would not be shocked by the contents of my letter. The magazine was called *Adogma*, remember? It purported to bridge the ideological gaps dividing our societies. A sort of planetary vision that stressed the basic elements common to mankind. Maybe the language was intended for nonhumans. I might have pitched too high. One day someone will recreate that order, tackling the matter more efficiently. If not soon, then undoubtedly in the next generation. In putting the magazine together I shouldn't have deviated from my original goal. Third Worldly in essence. Or should I? After all, don't I harbor irreconcilable traits, combining the fate of Western civilization with that of 'new' as well as 'old' emerging nations, among which one must count Israel. Israel whose every move is observed through a magnifying glass: a calamity and a privilege!

I am lying on the gravel, limbs spread out, offering the already bronzed surface of my skin to the sun's unwavering darts. Rasping sound of pebbles. She has arrived. I contract, bending my knees as if suddenly caught in the act of adultery. More than embarrassment, it is anger I feel. Anger at having been disturbed during a sacrificial ceremony where I perform the dual act of immolator and immolated. But before I can even slip on my trunks, Serena hands me an airmail letter, still sealed:

"It came just as I was leaving. Why would Sig. Giordano send mail by special delivery? . . . Yet I had told him . . ." she whispers to herself.

My fingers quiver. Should I let them loose and destroy the aerogramme? It would spare me further aggravation. A flurry of needles criss-crosses my stomach. The brain has awkward ways of calling us to reason. I rip the letter open, skim through its typewritten geometry and tear it into as many pieces as my fingers can manage. Serena's unsurprised stare. I then crumple the bits of paper with my other hand, release the grip and blow them off until they lie scattered on the beach like broken butterfly wings.

"Pretty, isn't it?" I remark.

"Anything important?" she asks, falsely lackadaisical.

"Maybe to him, but we shouldn't worry. That chapter is closed. Strange how conveniently you can rid yourself of unpleasant thoughts. I never believed I could do it."

A sigh, almost imperceptible, apparently one of resignation. Only in appearance! By now her wordless comments have become all too familiar. I wish she were a little more explicit. Her attitude is driving me crazy.

"Say something! I've upset you, haven't I? Tell me you hate my guts; tell me you want to . . . I've lost my mind."

Blank. She gropes in her deep straw bag. Clicking of a purse clasp.

"Take this," she urges commandingly.

Instead of a full answer, she gives me one of those knock-out sedatives prescribed by Dr. Fiorello. It leaves an unpalatable, dry taste on my tongue, as when you wake up in the morning before brushing your teeth. The medicine has a double effect; it puts me in an artificial state of elation—I giggle without wanting to—and works as a truth drug at the same time.

"Not much to conceal, is there—about Sig. Giordano?" I hear myself saying.

Sooner or later Serena catches up with my thoughts. At least, those involving decisions of a material order which we have in common. But nothing now prevents me from doing 'irresponsible' things, like writing to Sig. Giordano, or hurling my wristwatch to the ground one Saturday afternoon in the middle of Dizengoff Square.

A teenager bent down and was going to pick it up for me when I created a small panic among the strollers as I shouted:

"Look out!" The youth screamed like a betrayed puppy.

"A bomb, a bomb," echoed several voices.

The growing collective fear made me 'overreact'. All of a sudden the pole of attraction, I felt I couldn't draw back, and half-crying, half-cursing, I tramped on the watch hysterically, crushing it with my heel until the works burst out of its case.

"Meshugga!" someone jeered.

Then, slowly, the cluster of onlookers dispersed.

"Why don't you bathe in the nude?" I ask Serena, gazing at the cubic designs of her one-piece suit.

"You like it. Good for you. To each his own."

I was going to retort: "Is it prohibited by the feminist movement?"

But her tone froze my impulse. So cutting, so foreign to the Serena I know. A sense of shame gets hold of me. I, who've spent part of my summers in naturist resorts, suddenly come to a disturbing conclusion: she is sane, she doesn't need to exhibit herself!

# CHAPTER THREE

We're driving through the Negev desert in Dave's cramped Fiat 600. What a contrast between him and Shoshana, the Yemenite nurse he's brought along. He—typically mittel-europäisch; she—so dark, with very pronounced semitic features, and a trifle taller. Her bony profile seems to have been carved out of pumice stone. She was six months old when she and her family were evacuated from Sanaa, the capital of Yemen:

"We came to Eretz Israel in 1950 on the Magic Carpet."

By the way Shoshana smiles, I take it that's a pun.

"No, no," she insists on hearing Serena's incredulous chuckle,

"I'm not joking, that's what the Operation was called."

The nose is the most sensual part of her face, it has a life of its own, conforming with amazing elasticity to the subtlest change in expression. Her hair is a bundle of shiny ringlets uncovering a neck almost as spun-out as those of the giraffe-women. My hands quiver, longing to wrench that rubbery stem of flesh.

The clouds hang statically above us—a bleak watercolor smearing, hues of gray across every inch of the atmosphere—, from the desert sand to the Dead Sea. Even the air is flecked with slow-moving particles: light beads fallen from an invisible source, roaming aimlessly. I feel like one of those beads, lethargic and yet alive. But more than that, it is their false anonymity I identify with. Look at them! None is exactly the same. Few people have the patience to sort them out. They just can't be bothered yet remain dumbfounded when collisions occur above their heads, as if awakening from a catatonic trance.

Parts of the road are still flooded.

"We've had severe storms," Dave explains as we get out of the car, walking toward a brand new concrete building facing the sea. It's a thermal complex.

". . . good for rheumatism! Come on, let's have a dip," Shoshana says.

It's unusually cool for the season. I prefer it this way. Serena and Dave have decided to stay ashore. The water glistens like a huge oil puddle. Impossible to swim, it's so thick and gooey. Aren't we in the lowest spot on earth? The Pit and the Pendulum.

Three supine bodies loom in the near distance. Abdomens bulging over the surface like those bloated putrefying crocodiles I caught sight of one day on the shores of Lake Tanganyika. I don't like it here. The place has an apocalyptic flavor. Where did I read that the first Israelites might have been a tribe imported from another world, inhospitable and desolate, just like this place, where even a slim and desirable girl like Shoshana leaves me cold? We've assumed the color of the landscape: withered, dinosaurian. Brrr! I'm getting out.

"Wash off the salt immediately," urges my companion, somewhat disappointed that I left her floating in the magma—what else can you call it?

On our way back from the oasis of Ein Gedi—as refreshing to the eye as a turquoise half-buried in grime—we pick up a hitchhiker. I make space for him in the rear, squeezing myself up against Serena. He is a little fairer than our Yemenite nurse and has a cleft along the chin.

Dave and Shoshana begin a conversation with him in Hebrew. From what I gather his name is Fouad and he lives in Ramallah. During a moment of silence I notice the missing thumb on his left hand.

I ask him what kind of work he does, if he has a family. He shrugs his shoulders, indicating that he doesn't understand my language.

Dave interprets for us. We thus learn that he is one of seven sons of an Arab notable, that he refused to attend university like his brothers and chose instead to become a mechanic. That he doesn't believe there will be peace in Israel unless some kind of federation including the displaced Palestinians can be devised. That he realizes Jews are entitled to share this land, but only those who lived in the region before the British Mandate and the survivors of Nazi camps. Not the wealthy: they already enjoy a privileged status in their country of origin. He avoids mentioning Zionism. Serena introduces the problem of Russian Jewry.

Fouad's argument: "They represent a minority, just like the Armenians or the Uzbeks. I don't believe they are worse off than any of the others. Do they starve? Are they forbidden to attend schools? No! It's the political system, not a question of race. I'd like to see the world's reaction if all of a sudden the hundred and thirty-odd million Brazilians demanded to settle back in Portugal."

Shoshana intervenes: "You seem to overlook a major point. As a people, we have suffered more and much much longer than anyone else. And I am not underestimating the plight of the oppressed or the colonized. However, I do maintain that there is no parallel in history. Dogmas, you see, are a wonderful tool in the hands of our detractors, as malleable as clay. At one time it was convenient for them to blame the 'evils' of socialism on Jews. Today, a lot of people associate us with the capitalists, too readily. How would you define countries like Egypt, Lebanon, or Iraq—which by the way shows no particular tenderness toward its Kurdish minority? Then, there's a long ignored fact which the Arab countries are loath to remind anyone, lest they appear as the culprits that they actually were: after the birth of Israel, as many as one million Jews were expelled from their various lands, with nothing more than their suitcases to carry along. All of their properties were confiscated, their homes, their hard-won businesses and even their religious schools, when, if you remember, from your history books, Jews had lived in many of those countries before the Arabs came in to conquer the original folk—the Berbers and the Coptic Christians, who are both today discriminated against."

Our fellow passenger angrily retorts that that does little to justify Israel's denial of the Palestinians' rights.

He is right. Every human being on this planet deserves to be treated fairly and compassionately, and Israel ought to be ashamed of its treatment of a population that longs to live normally. Yet, what did all their rich brothers of Saudi Arabia, of the Emirates or of faraway Malaysia, do to better their plight, letting them rot for half a century in refugee camps in Lebanon, in Jordan or in Syria? And when the United Nations decreed that there ought to be two nations living side by side, why did the Arab countries unanimously reject the resolution, inciting the Palestinians to temporarily flee from their land, promising them to resettle on the whole territory after having thrown all the Jews into the Mediterranean?

The tension is mounting. Our car has suddenly become too cramped for such heated debate. Beads of perspiration rim Fouad's eyebrows. I feel his muscles throbbing against my flanks, and can almost hear his heartbeat. Or is it mine? That nerve on his temple! It is pulsating like the paunch of a baby lizard—so raw and diaphanous. It reminds me of the vivisection we had to perform during our last biology class, back in Africa. I had to excuse myself. Same feeling of faintness, same urge to throw up.

"Dave, please, stop the car, I need to . . . well, whatever . . ."

Nothing in sight but rubble and sand in this ugly Judean desert. Nowhere to escape, or hide. I choose a mound, about twenty meters off the road, and stay there a while, pretending to urinate, while I take another surreptitious glance at the scenery. Against all logic I decide to part company. Running away from that intolerable situation welling up in the Fiat 600, into the hinterland, where I might find some serenity. Amid the gravel and the stones. I wish I were petrified here and now, but I guess the miracle which struck Lot's wife won't repeat itself.

A honk. Another honk, this time prolonged. Bleating across the emptiness as it is in my entrails. I am a bouncing sound chest, purring and hiccupping like an ill-treated rag doll. In fact the noise seems to reverberate everywhere now. I don't even bother to look behind, conscious that someone is chasing after me and that I shall soon be caught. The honking resumes with intermittent wails. It gets weaker, and is soon replaced by the inevitable thud of human steps. I force to bring myself to a halt, wait, short of breath, arms dangling, until he comes and fetches me. He happens to be Fouad. The sinewy hand clutches my shoulder. "Why? Are you stupid?" exclaims the panting Arab.

Baffled at first, I break out into a convulsive sob and embrace him as though he has just risked his life for me. The coarse and virile smell of his perspiration seeps into my lungs like an invigorating gust of wind. I feel a gradual stiffening in his body: enough, it says, we are strangers. Yet I refuse to unclasp, for it is the only way I can communicate with him. How oddly does the flesh behave! His muscles are less taut, though I know his mind won't yield. If I could bend that obstinacy of his and let my thoughts gush forth! Telling him that we are blood brothers, that I cannot disagree with his reasoning, that he has transmitted to me the rancor of his people. That at this very moment my heart is dangerously swelling, like a transplanted organ subject to imminent rejection. For I do not want him to harbor any hateful sentiment against the Israeli Jews, or the others. He should, as I do, condemn terrorism, whichever side it comes from.

God! What is happening? Now he is clinging to me like an enraged animal. I feel the hardness at his crotch rubbing against my stomach. Furiously. While he tries to apply his mouth to mine. Grabbing me by the belt, he heaves me to draw us closer. His movements, frantic, knowing no restraint any more, give off the clapping sound of battered cowhide, while at the same time I am struggling to avoid contact with his face. And that . . . that missing thumb! At last, a deep, raucous cry spouts out of his throat. So powerful is the thrust that I lose my balance and drag him to the ground. We lie there for a moment, staring at each other. He, with fire in his eyes, lips half sealed with saliva, allowing an ultimate spasm to ripple through his body—real or feigned spurt of pleasure? I, aghast, still impregnated with the sour taste of tongue and sweat, uncertain whether what he has just done was a deliberate act of aggression to humiliate the 'enemy', or just a natural outburst.

A stain spreads around his fly like a blotch of ink. We exchange startled looks, looks of two people whose feelings waver between guilt, anger and compassion, forgetting who was the rapist and who was raped. Dave's nearing shouts prod us back to our feet.

"Are you both okay? I thought you were going to kill him!" he tells me as the Arab and I wink at each other.

During the rest of the trip I can't tear my gaze off Fouad, pondering on the audacity of his gesture. If he is capable of taking such a risk in broad daylight, I shouldn't be at all surprised that he indulges in activities of a much more serious nature. What a chasm lies between his sort of rebellion and mine! I imagine him slaying others while sacrificing his own life 'in the name of Allah'. Whereas I only seem to be able to hold myself to account for the hatred in the world.

Inattentive to Serena's caresses—she is stroking my knee—I keep staring at the young Arab, dwelling on bloody visions. His hard profile remains static. Perhaps he is concocting some kind of dangerous deed. Memories flash through my mind: the appalling sight of mutilated Hutus and Tutsis. It was in the hills of Burundi, after one of the worst ethnic outbreaks the country had experienced. And yet, that horror would be dwarfed in magnitude by the genocide that would sweep Rwanda in 1994. A friend and I were driving back to the capital when, passing a ditch, he enjoined me to stop the van:

"There! Something's moving!"

Only when we stepped out of the pick-up did we see a sample of the hushed-up atrocities that had occurred in the previous months. The thing my friend had noticed was a dog pawing at the remains of a human corpse. Seeing us, it had scurried away with shreds of dried flesh clasped in its fangs. Hairy black flies were circling the heap of dismembered bodies, while now and then a bumblebee would force its way into their midst, droning with impatience. What our eyes were exposed to was the result of ineffable savagery: a combination of medieval torture and Nazi mass disposal. Broken skulls emptied of their brains, severed heads and trunks, jaws transformed by axes, mouths stuffed with genital organs, countless impaled bodies. So unreal did this spectacle appear to me that even now I automatically shut it out of my consciousness, making myself believe it was the product of a screenwriter's sick imagination.

Hadn't as many as a quarter million people been slaughtered in the same gruesome manner, cut up in pieces, and shoved into similar ditches behind the hills of this beautiful land—the setting of a film entitled *King Solomon's Mines*, starring Stewart Granger and the lovely Deborah Kerr (or was it Ava Gardner?). Wasn't it also in the movies that I saw bloodstained desks and red puddles on the classroom floors? A school which strangely resembled the one I attended for six years!

Shoshana and our fellow-passenger are now conversing in Arabic. My fingers tightly interlocked with those of Serena, my eyelids bent by the whimsical strumming of the breeze, I savor the harsh cadences of this tongue.

What if, instead of me, it was Shoshana who had run away, farther, much farther into the desert? He would have stripped her first to the waist. She would've scratched and kicked him. He would've laughed, and then all at once, before she could even utter a sigh, he'd have devoured her with kisses. Her senses would finally burst out of their shell.

"Here's the bus station," Dave interrupts.

Fouad is already waving at us, with a smile that could be a grin. Dreams too are sometimes misleading!

# CHAPTER FOUR

We got the address of Dr. Bern through Mrs. Lindner's nephew. Serena insisted upon accompanying me to this first appointment. A session which is going to look like a game of musical chairs.

He invites her, alone, into his office. Meanwhile, I inspect the living room—rather spacious by Israeli standards. Or is it the bright woolen carpet and the Danish-style furniture which give this impression? An abstract painting signed 'Ellen Bern' monopolizes the only full length wall. Bookshelves, a glass-topped table with three chairs, half a dozen trinkets in stylized shapes, and a baseball lying under the TV stand.

My turn to be 'inspected': the doctor shows me in, and Serena out. So, he wants to hear the other side of the story! How many sides, to how many stories? I've been through that already in Milan, at least twice—I am not counting the woman-analyst I ran away from after fifteen minutes because she was twitching her hands as only an hysterical introvert does, nor the Schnauzer-faced psychiatrist who would doze off as I spelled out my case history—*eine kleine Nachtmusik* for his senile ears—and wake up clicking his tongue at the whirring sound of an invisible watch.

I have a hunch that this Dr. Bern, although full of good will, still has teething troubles: he purses his lips as if they were holding a straw—sipping at my words, perhaps. And also he frowns a lot for his age. However, deciphering a patient's lingo requires a good deal of mental effort; which I understand quite well. The contrast between his lustrous baby cheeks and a Newgate frill trimmed to perfection lends him an air of naivete. He's slightly older than me. Now and then, he jots down notes on a peach-tinted card. Color does add to life. I can almost see through his forehead. The task of 'skeletonizing' me is over. It just takes a receptive ear, and a goldplated pen—with, of course, a loaded cartridge.

He gets up, beckoning me not to move, and calls Serena in. We set up a schedule: three visits weekly. I insist that they be in the late afternoon, mainly because of the heat. He asks that I come alone. The bus stop is a mere five minutes' walk from his office. As he is about to dismiss us, Serena requests to see him in private. To her astonishment Dr. Bern politely, but firmly refuses:

"I'm sorry, from this point on, I'd like to keep it strictly between your husband and me."

She needs reassurance—about me, us, now, the near future—and he won't give it to her. She's out of the game.

Reduced to the role of spectator. The ghost of Sade lurks in me for a split second. Has she noticed the glimmer of triumph in my eyes? It evaporates into a thwarting realization: no one ever belongs to anyone else. It is the degree of this acceptance which proves decisive.

Our two lives are like streams of the same river, flowing parallel, rejoining from time to time. In which direction? Here lies the Great Dilemma, or might we say Gamble? We shall either part at the delta, and engulf ourselves in the treacherous currents of the sea, or aim at the source. All along, there are the tributaries, and perhaps one or more dams. But these remain secondary, since they constitute the inevitable array of hazards we have to expect under our sun. But then, too, we may be so short-sighted as to lose altogether our sense of purpose. And stall. As I have been doing for the past months. As I am doing right now, questioning my presence in this stranger's house. How pretentious of him to embark on my adventure! How weak of me to have accepted his participation! And Serena? All of a sudden I feel remorse for having excluded her. What new complicities will she be subjected to? None, for I do not intend to play the double agent. Aren't we, each of us, fraught with unknowns? Shrouded in halos of mystery? Some needing it as a protective sheath, others using it to confound their fellow men in order to escape their own ghosts, while others still, the so-called open books, disclose what is apparent to themselves, leaving out the unwritten.

The sun's glare ricochets from the tall white apartment blocks like a myriad of glistening needles. Serena puts on her smoke-rimmed glasses. I left mine home—I really hate wearing them. They have a hallucinatory effect on me: a screen between universes. Serena's give her an air of nonchalance befitting those jet set playgirls whose 'natural looks' are as synthetic as paper flowers. Yet she did ask my advice before picking the 'right ones'. At the time, I thought they were okay. What had disturbed me, I guess, was the optician's lofty attitude. I didn't like him and couldn't wait to get out of the store. So, it is partly my fault. In the beginning, she'd glance at me with an uncertain pout. I'd half reassured her: "One has to get used to them," or jokingly, "it's different, it's groovy."

But now, I'm developing an aversion to the image she projects: that of a *vita* euphemistically qualified as *dolce*. It's getting obsessive. I'm already seeing the army of reproachful eyes focused on her—on both of us. Is it because I deem this country too rough, a country which can only allow itself, as the ultimate luxury, subservience of the mind, however sophisticated, to physical labor, whether in the army or on the fields? Again, and more than ever, the words 'futility', 'superfluous' resound in me like screeching leitmotivs. And what about Dizengoff

Square's merry-go-round of the fashion-conscious Israeli youth?

The trip from Ashkelon to Dr. Bern's office—north of Tel Aviv—became such a hassle that after the third time, I refused to go. If it wasn't for Mrs. Lindner's idea that we should move to Netanya, I would have stopped consulting him, or for that matter any other analyst. Serena knows how much I loathe the impersonal, touristy atmosphere of hotels. Consequently, we are now renting, thanks again to the ingenious arrangements of Mrs. Lindner, a handsome studio which a relation of hers built as an independent annex for summer guests. A mere three hundred meters from Netanya's sparkling beach. For once, I don't mind staying at a popular resort town. Strolling along the broad and surprisingly uncluttered sidewalk cafés, I can't but think that the planners of this city went to places like Juan-les-Pins, in Southern France, or Lignano, on the Italian Adriatic coast, to glean a few tips. The result, though, in accent and flavor, is unmistakably Israeli—a travelogue description, huh!

Forgetting for a moment that we are not vacationers in the conventional sense, I drag Serena to the public gardens across the square. A group of puppeteers is entertaining children. They must be students. The girl is wearing a khaki outfit—a reservist no doubt. Pity, we've arrived at the end of the show. It's an apotheosis:

the repenting prince and warlord bow in front of a Council of Animals, taking the oath of allegiance to the goddess of peace—an orange-dotted ladybug. Riotous handclapping of little hands, punctuated by bravos of approval. Then sighs and gaping mouths when the puppeteers start packing. The spell so abruptly broken has cast a shadow of disillusionment on those still gleaming eyes. A lurking suspicion like that caused by a sudden awareness of betrayal. There is almost animosity in their looks now. The four entertainers have resumed the role of mortals, going about their daily preoccupations, as if they had nothing to do with the hands which created magic an instant ago. While the children disperse, one of the young men taps the girl on the shoulder and tells her with a lustful smile: "Tonight, Astrid, don't forget!"

Astrid: a resonance so rare and intimate that I feel it is almost a sacrilege when spelled in a stranger's mouth. Astrid: my beautiful mother, named after the diaphanous beauty who was Belgium's Swedish-born queen.

For a reason which I understood only much later, I never had the privilege, taken for granted by other children, of calling the woman who bore me 'mother'. Astrid was about sixteen when father started courting her. At that time she was attending the town's only Catholic girls' school. Religion had been her universe ever since she could remember.

From the early years at the mission, to 'Stella Mattutina', where kindly sisters strove to keep the souls of their protégés free of 'tropical temptations'. But temptation met Astrid one hot December evening. It bore the name of Orlando Romani. A pandemonium erupted when the 'Guardians of Morality' noticed a swelling under the teenager's white uniform. Something had to be done to avoid sullying the school's reputation. When father showed up, requesting the hand of his young mistress from the Mother Superior, a restrained sigh swept through the office. Restrained, because the two 'sinners' could not be wedded before the altar, but in the town hall.

Yes, father is a Jew—though he always tried to be discreet about it, considering himself an Italian to the core—but Jewish he is, nevertheless. The French language—we lived then in Belgian-ruled Africa—can be generous with euphemisms. Thus, when on rare occasions father had to remind an acquaintance or a customer that he was not a Christian, he'd mutter: "Je suis israélite." Juif has undertones of profanity, although in the phrase *Jésus, roi des juifs* it alliterates so well. Italian on the other hand boasts at least three variations, the 'noblest' being *israelita*, followed by *ebreo*, and, God forbid, *giudeo*. How miserably English compares in this instance: one is a 'good', or a 'bloody' Jew. One even 'jews down' his fellow men. And yet, logically enough, when applied to Christians, the degrees of evil remain contained within the boundaries of 'civilized' language. Doesn't 'dirty Christian' sound somewhat outlandish, farfetched? And how profuse, nay, luxuriant is the range of qualities encompassed in the 'saintly' term. Even in our permissive society one still hears such sweet ringing expressions as: "She displayed true Christian charity." "They sat down to a good Christian dinner." And, would you believe it? even a little poodle can be as smart as a Christian!

My beloved Astrid remained a devout Catholic during all of her short life. Was it because she had been parentless and given a home by the sisters? And a free education? Probably. Following my previous harangue, you may think that my attitude towards Astrid's benefactors is a nasty one. Cynical, perhaps, but not devoid of admiration. For after all, they did save her from death or at best from the grim existence shared by most half-castes. If it had not been for them, she might have 'sinned' more than once and become a street-walker. Instead, she met father. My cynicism, though, stems not from her experience, but rather from her insistence that I too should be blessed with the tenets of Christianity. I hold it no less against her husband for having gone along. Thus, I spent nine years, counting the pre-school Montessori classes, in an atmosphere impregnated with

Pater Nosters, the scent of incense and omnipresent friars whose odor followed me right home, creeping at night under the sheets of my bed. I was so accustomed to the virile smell of perspiration that emanated from their heavily starched robes that when I switched to the co-ed *Athenée*, I felt something was missing, something which couldn't be readily spotted, as when you forget to brush your teeth.

Astrid's complexion had the quality of matte porcelain. I would burn to hug her, flinging my arms around her neck, but at the last moment, as if held back by invisible claws, I'd stroke her cheek with the tip of my lips, closing my eyes to inhale the fragrance of lavender she wore so naturally. Father must have loved her to a degree bordering on obsession, for he was constantly, nerve-wrackingly aware of her every move or gesture, when in front of strangers. Even at the office—Astrid did the bookkeeping and would occasionally lend customers a hand as an interior decorator—he'd discreetly pass her a remark about her dress or her make-up. They often used to quarrel at home because of that. He'd harp on the same things over and over again, while Astrid would stand up to him like a tigress. Contrary to what most people thought—in public she'd avoid his stare, hardly flinching at all—my mother was a strong-willed and very stubborn woman. She even slapped him a couple of times, behind the sanctuary of our private walls; overwhelmed, he'd look at her as if she were an apparition.

One evening Astrid called me to the veranda. There was something unusually calm in the tone of her voice; father was stretched on his lounge-chair, relaxed while sipping at a glass of *anisette*.

"So, how did it go today, boy?" he asked me as I sat down.

"Well . . . as far as I know," I replied as my gaze flitted back and forth, from him to Astrid. I got jittery when I saw my mother raising her eyebrow, and confused.

"What I am about to say is pretty serious; I'd like you, Alexis, to listen very attentively."

Thoughts flashed in my mind like sparks bouncing in a kaleidoscope. Then, when they all faded out, with the exception of one, I had the sensation of a rod burning in the area of my spine. I shuddered at the assumption that the principal might have learned about my relationship with Mademoiselle Lombard, our history teacher, and reported it to my parents. Could such a thing be explained, let alone understood?

But to my surprise and to father's even greater astonishment, he was the target, not I. Leaning forward, the glass still clutched in his hand, he listened, mesmerized, to Astrid's 'revelation'.

"If it hadn't been for you, Alexis, I'd have divorced your father long ago. Oh, he's very kind and generous.

Take a look at my wardrobe: there is hardly a dress or tailored suit without a designer label. He's selected each one of them."

"What's wrong with that? You are a beautiful creature and I want you to look your best."

Almost ignoring what he'd just said, she continued in a cold monotone: "The problem, Alexis, is that I can't and do not wish to hide my origins. Your father has never been explicit about it—he's too tactful for that—but in a thousand ways he reminds me that I am a *métisse*."

"You're being unfair, Astrid, if this were the case, would I have married you at all?"

As I attempted a conciliatory nod at father, her voice became hoarse with anger:

"It is much subtler than it appears. You're old enough to understand, Alexis. Being a *métisse* in this country is not very flattering. We are considered . . . well, women with low morals."

At that moment father turned livid and mumbled, apologetic: "It's to protect you."

"So there we are: *Monsieur* Romani feels pity for his wife and tries to excuse her for what she is. I know what you Jews have been through but, Orlando, please if we must stay together then do spare me those persecution tantrums of yours. I won't take them any more. Then, addressing me again:

"I wanted to warn you, Alexis, for I do not wish you to suffer unduly later on. You are part of me: a half-caste, and part of him, a Jew. In any event, be proud of yourself. Pride is a necessity, not a luxury.

# CHAPTER FIVE

Fifth session with Dr. Bern. He inquires about my sexual activities while casting a sideways glance at my crotch. I have the same white shorts on I used to wear during my last school year in Africa. Not until I left for Italy did I get accustomed to regular pants. As he is listening, giving an occasional nod, the tip of his tongue brushes his fleshy lips in long-drawn strokes. His mouth is now glistening with lust, like a ripe cumquat dipped in syrup. I can almost sense the gurgling behind his Adam's apple as if suddenly my words have become a fluid substance injected down his throat. Clearly, he envisions the act of fellatio. I'm enjoying what I see, impishly, certain this time that my so-called ailment totally escapes the brilliant young analyst. Both he and the likes of him! Paying scant attention to my wry smile, he concludes:

"Well, you're able to swim, sleep, eat and even indulge in lovemaking. It isn't all that negative, is it?"

I stare at him meekly, somewhat unnerved. What can I add to this? It would be useless to tell him how simplistic I find his statement. Maybe I should take into consideration the environment in which he operates. He's probably served at the front, on the Lebanese border, or even in Gaza; dealt with a number of casualties: blind soldiers, maimed civilians.

This constant empathizing only accentuates my despondency. I get up to take leave of Dr. Bern, wondering if I should let him know.

"Farewell." I believe he heard me. But of course, no word is taken at face value. We are caught up in the semantic maze. What is meaningful, or meaningless? And everybody at one time or another has that itch to run up against a dead end—it's a vogue, a long-lasting one, institutionalized by Freud, Fritz & Co. It's become more of an addiction really. People no longer dare to talk their hearts out.

I told him: "Farewell." It could just as well have been: "I don't trust you," or . . . "Fuck off!" The road from snobbism to vulgarity is as smooth as a highway knifing the desert, with its mirages of glistening parodies. Too many of us find ourselves trapped in illusions, thinking we have reached the ultimate. How perilous and inept! So we awaken, not once, but each time we are undone by our own dreams, concealing our astonishment behind those masks the Greeks used in their plays. Apparently, much has changed in human attitudes since ancient times. Our minds have developed defense mechanisms to ward off the merciless intrusions of Technogods, while our nervous fibers respond like an outdated machinery gone wild. Never has man striven so hard to break through the repression of feelings. Take Dr. Bern. Not only does he feel empathy for me, but he's dying to have a taste of my flesh. Even our vocabulary, in spite of the thousands of newly-coined words, is inadequate, and the gap seems to be widening. Nowadays you so often hear the expression: to love-hate a person, or a city. Haven't the lexicographers been able to find a less ambiguous term? On the other hand, how sophisticated and poetic 'laser' sounds!

'Farewell': it bears a somewhat ludicrous connotation. When I said it, I meant that I did not wish to see him again. Which doesn't exclude the possibility that I might change my mind, or that our paths may cross again one day—in an unpredictable time and place.

Tonight Serena wants us to go out with a college friend of hers she bumped into the other day. We are meeting him in Safad, at the artists' colony. On our way there she presses my hand in silence, as if to prove something. Jealousy has never been a problem between us, but I'm so susceptible now that the slightest gesture on her part irks me. I withdraw my hand.

"Don't worry," she whispers.

I look around to see if our fellow passengers on the bus are watching us. The little boy across the aisle must not like the way I'm staring at him. He lifts his elbow in an obscene manner, suggesting that I should go and . . . I suddenly forget his age and barely repress a fit of anger. I hear whispers again—the voice of reason:

"He's just a child, Alexis!"

If that is intended to echo my conscience, damn all the Serenas of the world. No, on this count I'm wrong: someone is overreacting. But the little brat over there keeps putting on faces. Age! Age my foot. He needs a good smack. What makes him so different from me? The fact that he shows his disapproval openly—who gave him permission?—what I am not allowed to do? Of course, no one in his right mind would admit that most of us so-called adults yearn for the privileges of lost childhood. And when such yearning is manifested, we are ridiculed. But aren't Americans still very much looked down upon as overgrown children by the old country folks? After all, they're so . . . boisterous! And what of the Africans who "will never grow up"!

Well, look at the brat, look at what he is doing with his fingers, rubbing them together while stretching his neck towards Serena who is busy filing her nails.

"Madam," I grunt. Loud enough to catch the attention of the woman I presume to be the brat's mother. She's noticed the boy's gesture and twists his ear. Shrieks of a bat. The brat! Sometimes, I wish I could, by a stroke of magic, obliterate from sight all those obnoxious creatures who in a few seconds are capable of spoiling a whole journey. There should be some privacy. Curtains, or something. But public transportation has little respect for the individual!

Walking up and down the narrow alleys of Safad. Cobblestones and grit façades, with a rare wooden balcony at the curb; one of those moucharabeys whose latticework has hidden generations of languishing eyes, revengeful plots—Allah only knows how many. Even now, against the amber-flecked twilight, it is rippled with unholy shadows.

Serena's college friend signals us to pause while he gauges the structure with the angle of his thumb and forefinger. Jerry is an architect of Irish descent. Sexy, ruffled hair, outrageously auburn for a man. A head that strikes you like one of nature's rarities. Which makes it difficult to settle on a qualifier. 'Handsome' somehow does not fit, or 'beautiful'. It's like something you have to adjust to.

A Moorish cellar. Pargeted walls smelling of freshly coated plaster. The aperture carved at street level, grilled with thick iron bolts; the hooks hanging low from the vaulted ceiling suggest that this might have served once as a torture cell. How loathsomely we humans often react, without so much as feeling a pinch of remorse.

Enjoying instead the quaintness of a place which exudes memories of cold sweat and muffled supplications—I hear shackles grinding. A dungeon is infinitely more romantic than those brassy cafeterias that dot the continents from Kinshasa to Bangkok. In an era in which discrimination has become an untreatable virus, as elusive as the cause of cancer, the nostalgic aesthete in us looms up indiscriminately, with a color blindness everyone seems to excuse. And why? Because, whether we repress it or not, we are morbidly attracted to things past. The ugliness of other times is looked upon with complacency, if not outright admiration. Return to the source. Find your roots and plough them back into a richer soil. But what if you're endowed with wings? It's a matter of outlook: the bird's-eye view as against subterranean prying—by the way, I have great respect for moles.

The three of us seated around a gate-leg table, facial expressions colored by the whimsical-erotic games of a flickering candle. Jerry's forehead shines like the glazed surface of chestnut frosting, especially now when he's frowning. When they embraced an hour ago, he lifted her in a brotherly fashion. A fashion to which Serena responded with incestuous elan. They twirled and kissed in synchronized harmony such as only a pair of dancers are capable of—or two people whose limbs are magnetically sealed to each other from the moment they meet. The bear hug, his broad smile couldn't fool me.

In fact, I believe he was sincere, as he is at the present moment. Considerate too. He doesn't seem the type who'd want to meddle in other people's affairs. Only, Serena is not just another person to him. Look at his profile. The contour of his lips. So full and moist, it's a crime not to assuage them. And I know Serena wouldn't have committed such a crime. The furrow underlining his cheekbone is a scar, which instead of hardening his features accentuates the boyish quality in him. A tall, smooth-skinned boy with ruffled auburn hair.

"Right now, I'm working on a housing project in San Diego. I came here to gain a better perspective. What impresses me most, after Moorish architecture, is the Herodian period."

She is listening with an arched eyebrow, at once intent and frustrated. I too am wondering about the kind of life he leads—his private life, that is.

". . . a blending of two different styles: the Mexican colonial and the medieval, but in a modern context, that's what I'm aiming at."

The blending, the fusion of two bodies, perhaps three: Jerry, Serena and . . .

"Last year Alexis and I thought of taking a trip to the West Coast and driving all the way to Colorado. We had to cancel it a week before. KBI—his firm—sent him to the Persian Gulf instead. One of those urgent contracts, you know."

The latter part of Serena's remark was addressed to me in a tone very unlike hers. There was something derisive about it. It must be the presence of Jerry. Here comes her hand again—comforting warmth—over mine. The way she pronounced KBI suddenly throws light on the main reason for my wanting to quit the company. A reason which I couldn't until now quite define. I've often brooded about those three letters. KBI, Unilever, Aramco. They all share that ambiguous notoriety long-established trademarks inspire among the public and from which insiders draw their pride. Shuffle the letters, or change a couple, and KBI readily acquires a more official, awesome connotation. In a way, it is so akin to FBI or . . . KGB, in sound if not in purpose—but who am I to make such assertions? At KBI, world trade is the master word, and all the people we sign contracts with are VIP's. A notion good old Signor Giordano assiduously reiterated, lest I dump it somewhere along the way, in my countless missions abroad.

"Your job must be quite rewarding. In a sense, aren't you a goodwill ambassador?" Jerry observes, colliding head on with my train of thought. I take umbrage and retort that it is no honor to be the accomplice of a gravedigger, however resplendent the tombstone may appear, and if that's his opinion of multinational companies, we ought to change the subject of conversation.

His hands fan out in a sudden gesture of disbelief, his mouth agape, forming a pigeonhole. But the surprise comes from Serena.

"Enough," she bursts out, "I won't have it, and spare me the excuse of your depression, will you? As a matter of fact, I demand an apology." Waving his hands again, but this time vigorously, Jerry mutters: "Please . . . let's not make a fuss."

What a pair of hands can do! They've quieted us both down, Serena and me. But the atmosphere will remain tense throughout, there's no helping it. I'll try to control myself by not uttering another word. It's not good for us, an explosion is bound to ensue when we are back in our room. They've resumed their conversation, talking almost in whispers, and glance at me every once in a while. Jerry's eyes glimmer like those of a lion cub, sensually mischievous and pleading at the same time. My presence, or rather the lack of it, makes him feel uncomfortable. The mood is peculiar. When I look at Serena, I have the feeling that I am intruding in some prohibited sphere, into a past where I am unwelcome. Yet when he stares at me, the way he's doing now, a faint smile hung over his upper lip, Serena becomes the intruder, not I.

He is the first person, since we have been married, who has aroused in Serena the demon of jealousy. She is taking sides, protecting herself against my present fragility. All of a sudden it dawns upon me that she too needs an outlet. And seeing the man with whom this can be made possible, I feel relieved and, unexpectedly, devoid of any sense of possessiveness, say:

"Jerry, I'd appreciate it if you both spent some time together, alone. You'd do me a favor. How about tomorrow?"

Serena gives me a blank stare. She is used to my being unpredictable, a trait which, before my 'illness', she seemed to enjoy. But now that I'm getting out of bounds her attitude has changed.

"That isn't funny, Alexis," she concludes.

No use trying to convince her. As for Jerry, I know he believes me, I am positive. Of course, it's not up to him to take the initiative. Let's leave it at that. We shall meet again during the week, and maybe Serena will accept my proposition as an honest one.

"I'm through with Dr. Bern."

Serena made no comment, yet she looked somewhat disillusioned. It wasn't so much that I would cease to be under the care of a therapist—I had already dropped hints to that effect on several occasions, pointing out his 'shortcomings', but that I wanted to leave this town and go back to Mrs. Lindner's pension in Ashkelon where, in my retreat, down below the cliffs, I would feel less estranged. This meant that we wouldn't be able to see as much of Jerry as we had in the last two weeks.

"Do you really think you'll be better over there?" she asked, then, as if suddenly stung, said "No, it's too isolated. I won't take the risk."

She was so determined that I threatened to pack at once and make a go of it alone. A bitchy thing to do, but I couldn't help it. After having quarreled the whole morning, I said, in a subdued tone that which she couldn't voice, without doing injury to her pride:

"We'll find a way to keep in touch with Jerry. He can always join us for the weekends."

Contrary to appearances, my proposition was neither nasty nor magnanimous. Selfish at best, for I had grown used to him, almost addicted. The problem was that we never managed to see each other alone—he and I. This in part, and the excuse of dropping the analyst, prompted me to return to Ashkelon.

Then too, there is something else. Not until Jerry's existence and his previous ties with Serena were revealed to me had I noticed that streak of pain glowing in her eyes, like the opening of an old wound. Where is the scar hidden? I don't believe she will tell me, except that now I am sure it is somehow linked to Jerry. The way she's been acting with him—small incidents here and there. More than once I gave them the opportunity to go out together, on their own. Each time she found a pretext not to and, yes, almost panicked at the idea.

Yesterday we did not leave the room at all. Around three in the afternoon Mrs. Lindner came up and knocked at the door to see whether we were all right. Serena told her it was just one of my days and that she shouldn't worry. We made love so many times, with such passion—or rage—that by early night we had fallen exhausted on the bed, as over a field where the sole witnesses that remain of an annihilating battle are smouldering cinders. It had indeed the taste of a battle, unlike the sensuous love of our honeymoon seven years ago. Only the gestures, the strokes reminded us of the past.

I was awakened by a thunder-like blast, sprang to my feet and caught a glimpse of a jet squadron raking dawn's purplish horizon in three splendid trails.

Eyes beatifically veiled, the copper splash of her mane over both pillows, and her arm bent as if to form an alcove, Serena still appears to be dreaming. Aren't her secrets unfolding behind those lids? Decanting like a mellow wine trapped for years in a cellar? Hours ago, just before I collapsed, drenched with feminine fragrances and the odor of musk and sweat, it occurred to me that our thoughts had since the very first instant wandered in the same direction—bodies clasped together, but with Jerry on our minds. We had both loved by proxy, and now as I watch her, slowly slipping out of her sheets—protective sheath—I feel a pang inside, as well as the urge to escape.

I wash up, leaving my hair unkempt, put on a pair of sponge trunks and an Arrow shirt, and off I go.

"Last night was fabulous," I whisper, shutting the door behind me. It's much too early to bathe, so instead of heading towards the cliffs I take the path across the scrubby expanse north of the city proper. There are landscapes, like this one, so familiar to the senses that you wish never to have to leave them. I recognize a snake pit at my feet. It's half covered with scorched weeds. With the heel of my sandal I pound the earth near it until I can hear that hollow sound which has so often made me shudder. This time it is shudders of pain/pleasure coursing through my veins. I need not seal my eyes entirely. The shores of my youth are at a stone's throw. Those of majestic Lake Tanganyika.

Lapping of the waves. Rustling of the leaves. Cantilena of the rushes through a bamboo curtain. Linear harmony. Threatening like a dense formation of long-bladed spears. Like an army of skeletons standing at attention. While the cicadas fill the air with their strident crackle. Black Aphrodite's—that's what they call this gloomy place. We're in a blind alley, surrounded by a ditch. Beyond the faint light of a petroleum lamp stretches the bush, to darkness and infinity. But within the cob wall huts strange noises can be heard, equivocal sounds which already give me the creeps. Why did I follow that stinker of a Jose? Have I acted in full awareness, that I should inflict upon myself such punishment? I've no censor named God, yet the idea of committing a reprehensible act haunts me. I'm obsessed by what people define as evil or sin. As in a volcanic eruption that spreads its nacreous fluid around its crater, I feel the lava simmering down to my entrails. Mass of nerves, locked and intertwined. I'm burning to flee. But what is keeping me nailed to this place, also known as 'Ebony Pigalle'? Normal curiosity, or the thirst of a potential sex maniac? I can't stand Jose, least of all Jose the 'initiator'. I could very well have found a pretext to stay at home. No! The responsibility lies with my own yearnings and repressed dreams.

"Get a little closer! I'll show you how to handle those negresses!" Imbecile! Has he forgotten that I am the son of a colored woman? Murmurs, punctuated by a hushed wail, as if springing from an invisible fountain. A twig cracks near us. Other sounds. Indistinct. At times reminiscent of the swishing of clothes. Reunion of beings from another planet.

I shiver. What just crept under my feet? Those eerie noises again. Flare-up of the imagination. Reality through a magnifying glass. My English teacher writing a name on the blackboard: Loch Ness. A hydroid monster taking shape. Not the one I once saw in a mythology book. An African dragon, with a crocodile's tail, two huge mandibles grafted on its gills, mouth of a hippo and fins that unfold like the wings of a giant bat. The air is sticky and tepid. I feel glued in a nightmare. Then, as if to celebrate the final sinking of the sun, a formidable cry rends the atmosphere: "Aaaa . . . Illah, Aaaa . . . Illah, Aaaa . . . Ilah!"

My hand clutches Jose's arm. He too got a fright. I sensed it in spite of his puffing like the braggart that he is. A flicker of fear. Of course, he wouldn't admit it.

"Did you hear that? An Arab who's just come. You know, they're circumcised, those bastards. They really enjoy their fucking."

I hear myself answer, despondently:

"Listen, Jose, couldn't we leave . . . do this another day . . . ."

"You're not chickening out, are you? Don't worry, they won't eat you. Too busy screwing. This is the United Nations in miniature. U.N. by night! Every nationality. Just name it. Belgians, Greeks, oh, by the way, I saw Yanaki here last time. Wow, did he have a ball! What was I saying? Oh, yeah! There are also Indians, Ishmaelites—you know, those who worship the Aga Khan—the whole lot! And now . . . an Italian."

With feigned flippancy I inquire:

"What about the Blacks? Do they also come here?"

"No, they're not allowed in this joint. Can't afford it either. All the dough goes to the Arabs. Pimps. Enough talk! Let's get a move on. Act, man, act. Monique's waiting for us. A real alley cat. Fourteen years old. And juicy like a ripe mango. Hold it! I'll go see first."

Should I take advantage of my temporary solitude? The road is just a few meters away. I'd only have to jump over the ditch and I'd be free. Free from this nauseating adventure. But I lack the courage. My feet refuse to obey. Anxiety. Panic. Can't even bear the slow panting that has replaced my breath. Mummified. Almost wished now Jose were by my side! A scorpion could sting me, I wouldn't be able to utter a sound. Swear words. A fight breaks out behind the thicket:

"May the nioka (snake) impale you! You slut! May it guzzle your ovaries, twist your insides!"

Someone chortles. A sorrowful voice answers. That of a child: "Don't hit me, bwana Mohammed, please. I Promise, I won't do it again. Here, take the eighty franga (francs). It's the count, I swear to God."

"Little bitch you, whore. Daughter of a whore, granddaughter of a whore!"

A light tap on my shoulder. Jose's come back. A very young girl stands by his side. She tilts her head, looks fidgety. Bare and arrogant breasts. Firm nipples protruding like two specks of coffee on a silky black skin, with a strong odor of semen. Hair bunched up in tiny plaits. Bruised neck, visible through the darker patches. I want to avoid her stare but can't. So innocent, and yet inviting. At the same time fraught with womanly perversion.

"How much?" asks Jose. "Ingapi, I said. Are you deaf?"

"A hundred," she mutters.

"*Masimu*, you're mad, completely mad," he retorts with an obscene gesture.

"Then ninety, bwana."

"Look here, cherry blossom, I'll pay you fifty francs, but him," pointing in my direction, "it's his first time. Seventy-five for both of us! Do you hear? Now take it, it's an order."

"Okay, bwana Jose," she whimpers.

Addressing me, Jose groans: "C'mon, down to work! Aren't you craving to taste that little pussy?"

His attitude, the language he uses, the haggling, as if it were goods on sale. All this repels me. That women should sell their flesh, that sex should be bought like a vulgar crate of poultry, that each part of their body should be weighed and earmarked like veal carcasses hanging in a cold storage chamber ready for the butcher's, can only be a diabolical plot devised thousands of years ago.

One idle afternoon, I went rummaging through father's private shelves and found a volume, illustrated with tantalizing etchings: Famous Courtesans, the Sidelines in the History of Europe's Royalty. Dozens of pictures showing ladies lolling back on sumptuous beds, in the most lascivious poses. Vaporous blouses, long skirts with frills, muslin gowns, flowing robes. There they were: the peoples of Ancient Greece, the stolas of haughty Roman noblewomen, the Purple Hem of a Byzantine empress, the tight, bell-shaped dresses of all the Pompadours, the crinolines and the puffed sleeves of the Augsburg patrician ladies, the cloak and diadem of austere German princesses and the more sophisticated lace-trimmed mantillas of Spanish Damas. But of all those beauties, I see no other approaching the sensual simplicity of Pauline Borghese, stretched out on a divan, expecting her lover with that unfathomable, irresistible self-assurance of the Bonapartes. Thus do I envision the prelude to the love that one buys. And I abhor that sort of love, for the word itself strikes out all thoughts of base material considerations. Too sacred a notion to be tarnished by money. Only when I see Botticelli's Venus is love incarnated: hair that tumbles down like a shower of golden dew, flesh so ethereal that it would be sinful to touch it, a face enigmatic and yet incredibly soothing. Midnight Ladies, women caged up in netless aviaries, poetically called 'Dove's Nest', 'Le Bateau Ivre', or 'Diana's Arc', names I've picked up in father's *Addresses for a Lonely Gentleman.* Paris, Vienna, Florence, prestigious capitals where the colorful, often bloodstained patchworks of history have been woven . . . behind heavy cretonne curtains, in bowers exhaling suave fragrances, the intimate scent of lace undergarments . . . angel skin, orange flower, vetiver water, lavender . . .

Odor of wild fowl in the hut, smell of cassava and beer mixed with millet. Stench of perspiration. Musty. Like butter turned rancid. Like a whiff blown from a nearby sewer. My lungs hurt. Want to cough. Spit it all out.

Here we stand, the three of us, bent over in this mud hut that a tornado could wrench away in seconds. And this dizzying, musky smell of copulation. How many men have thrust themselves upon her, battering those young thighs? Dwindling glimmer of a candle stump. Shadows of our ghosts.

"Take off your kitenge!"

The girl unfastens her loincloth with surprising swiftness and lets it glide to the ground, like a snake sloughing its skin. She has a slender figure, superb curves—they don't go with her baby face. I'm ashamed to gaze at her.

"Lie down! *Mbio*! Quick, I said!" Suddenly Jose's tone has changed. His voice is much softer. Never have

I seen him like this. Even his eyes, usually so hard and cynical, have a different glow now. He turns around and reaches out a brotherly hand to me:

"Touch, Alexis, touch. Feel how warm it is."

I'm shaking. I dare not respond. And Jose, sensing it, takes my hand with caution. Reassuring gestures. I resist. He persists. He eventually draws me closer. I kneel down. My fingers are in a rapture. They fondle a stiffening breast. The nipple swells like the tip of a balloon. It palpitates and makes my heart leap with new sensations. Pale hand, black breast. One same beat. I think of Tahiti and Gauguin's *vahinés*. Isn't Monique one of them? The palm of my hand becomes moist. Moist with pleasure. I feel the throb of the areola, that flower of flesh exuding, I imagine, drops of honey. Flash of lightning across the mind: that grotesque bookmark I used to keep in my first-grade drawer at school; the obese farmer resting on a log in the middle of a field, milking his cow. Udder . . . teats . . . how much more 'noble' is the bosom of a girl as lovely as Monique! Yet, the treatment she gets is no better than that of an animal. They'll use her for as long as she can earn them a profit. Until she's completely dry. If I had the power, I'd have them lined up against a wall and shot in an endless row. But I have fallen in their net, like one of those meaty *banga-banga* fish our cook serves us on Friday evenings. I hate myself for being here. And hate Jose. Too late now, I can't escape.

I'm getting an erection. I'm dying to make love to that girl, to feel the velvet between her thighs, the lukewarm embrace of her labia . . . tightening around my sex. Rings of flesh trundling up and down with serpentine elasticity. Gushes of love fondling a virgin penis. Oh, I'm going to come, I'm straining myself to halt the orgasmic outburst, as long as I can. Unbearable, oppressing pain. Then an overpowering release.

"Alexis, move away, will you? Let me fuck her. The bitch, she's all wet."

Mind in a total haze. My eyes are a blur. I'm watering from every pore. Shaking like a tree caught in a flood. All of a sudden the beast—curiosity—is again unleashed. Laying its paws around my neck, shutting me up like a wild bird in a zoo cage. Eyes wide open. Lucidity recovered. All senses concentrating in the optic nerve. Jose unzips his fly. Pushes the girl flat on the mat. Bends over his prey, covering her waist and breasts. Pants out words, which in his mouth sound paradoxical. Like a poem inserted by mistake in an accounting book.

". . . let thy middle gape . . . quench my thirst for love . . . so frail, my dove . . . let me in your kingdom . . . see how strongly it wants you . . . bird of Eden . . . drink of my fountain of youth . . . sacred, sacred womb . . . thou shalt beget Africa's handsomest prince . . . ."

Jolts of bodies in lubricated oneness. He writhes like a lion wounded in its loins by a poisoned arrow. Ultimate, shattering thrust. Then a groan, resembling the death rattle, gradually fading in a gasp. Sudden convulsion. That of a freshly beheaded victim. Until the Portuguese finally collapses. Toneless, extinguished voices. Did I say voices? I can't remember her uttering a word all the while they were making love. What could she be thinking? Could it be . . . nothing?

I feel sticky between the legs. A large ring stains my khaki shorts. It's over. Jose stands up.

"That was good. This whore is unbeatable, man!"

Why does he have to spoil everything? A whore! There's the real Jose, the seducer, the bragging deflowerer of vestals.

"Here, take this! It's a condom."

He sickens me. I come up with some foolish excuse.

"She, worn out? Are you kidding? Fucking is her business. And nobody asks her opinion."

The way he puts it. When I think that just a few minutes ago he spoke so . . . softly, so compassionately. Where has the dove disappeared? What has become of the bird of Eden? She remains mute. And yet she doesn't look at all unhappy, or even vexed. Could that mean indifference? Apathy? Whirlwind of images once more. Cage. Prison. No, I won't wear that contraceptive. Anyway, not in front of Jose. Why the hell doesn't he go? I've already had an orgasm. All alone. But she excites me, terribly. Venereal disease. Syphilis. I'm terrified and suddenly find myself yelling: "Let me out of here!"

They both stare at me. With awe. Then with astonishment. No use insisting. Jose understands. He shakes the girl and orders her to give him back twenty-five francs.

"But there were the two of you in the hut. What will Bwana Mohammed say?"

"That's your problem. Goddamn it! He didn't screw you, did he!" "Please . . ." I mumble.

"Give it back or I'll beat you like he's never done it before, your Bwana Mohammed. And if you go on, I'll tear your *cuma* (cunt) apart." Those smells of sated flesh and perspiration. That taste of vomit tickling the back of my tongue. I'm ready to burst. And I do:

"Will you stop harassing her? Here's the change. Now let me get out of this place!"

# CHAPTER SIX

The heads of several Black African States have hinted that "if the oil-producing nations do not abide by their promises to help them financially, they shouldn't be surprised if some of us reconsider our policy toward Israel' . . . ."

I crumple the paper into a tennis-sized ball and wonder what Astrid would have thought of it if she were alive. I remember how nervous and susceptible she became in the months following Burundi's independence. The debacle of our neighboring giant, Zaire, was continuing to send us shock waves and to scare the population in spite of the new government's reassurances. The spectacle of the refugees pouring into our town—first the Europeans and later the Congolese who had escaped tribal massacres—left a taste of foreboding on everyone's lips whenever the subject was broached.

What a far cry from the initial days of rejoicing, after the green, red and white flag, studded with three Stars of David, had been hoisted, replacing the colors of Belgium! Rumors of coups and countercoups circulated in hushed table conversations. They crept under closed doors like insidious gas leakages. In fact, the whole town was overrun by them. Distrust settled among the township and city dwellers alike, regardless of race or political inclination. We were being plagued by a ubiquitous virus: spy-o-mania. And contrary to what outsiders might have believed, those who feared this epidemic most were not the Europeans, whose presence in a country as poor as ours was considered a gift, however indigestible, but rather the local people. It was the Hutu majority, in particular, who found themselves trapped once more—after Belgium's fifty year intermezzo—under the yoke of the handsome Watusi aristocrats.

Practically overnight, our tiny melting pot of a city—Burundians here were outnumbered by foreigners—turned into a full-fledged capital. Embassies sprouted everywhere. Though some later closed down, after the authorities had deemed them dangerous to the country.

Anyway, this new state of affairs kept father quite busy. As a building contractor, that is. The very nature of his business helped confine us among the politically innocuous, while at the same time we were permitted to savor the *gourmandises* of diplomatic circles. A smorgasbord of sorts, filled with the ingredients of fascination and pettiness—pleasantly sweet at first, becoming somewhat cloying as the palate got more sophisticated, but then again delectable. This was the kind of atmosphere Astrid had to adjust to before departing this volatile world of ours.

Late one afternoon, driving back from the swimming pool on my motor scooter, I found Astrid sunk in an armchair, wiping off smeary blotches of mascara under her reddened eyes with the corner of a tissue. She must have broken down in one of her solitary fits, but now she didn't even bother to conceal it. Instead, she clutched at the armrest as if trying to resist a force that wouldn't let go. She needed an outlet; and uncharacteristically—as in that confession several months earlier when, for the first time in my presence, the word divorce had been uttered—she opened up again.

"He's using me as a pawn, Alexis. It's ten times worse than before Independence."

I suddenly wished I'd never been her son. The way her liquid eyes pleaded with me indicated that she too longed for some kind of metamorphosis which, however illusory, would undo the knotted ties of kinship between us.

"I haven't a single friend in this bloody world. Not even a woman friend," she stressed, making me feel for a split second an antagonistic representative of the 'stronger' sex.

"In fact, there is someone, or rather was: Natasha Makharova. I met her at one of those exasperating cocktail parties your father insists that I attend. We fancied each other immediately, and I'd go and get her after work at the Soviet embassy. We used to drive towards the old airstrip or up in the hills, past the evangelical mission. She wasn't very talkative, but some of the things she said touched a chord in me I had thought dead long ago. She lost both her parents during the Stalin era. How and why, she never explained. Then, as if suddenly realizing she had been carried away, she'd apologize for being over-sentimental and stare at me, frowning until I'd smile again. She was a wonderful listener and I used to forget how far apart our worlds were—that she was raised in a socialist society and that in appearance we had so little in common. Yet, I don't remember, even during my school days, having felt so close to another person. Natasha knew many intimate things about me, but was tactful enough not to make any comments when . . . well . . . what's the use. It's all over anyway. I never understood much about politics except that it succeeds in spoiling many a beautiful relationship. The fact remains that I miss her terribly. Oh, we do see each other now and then, but she's turned as frigid as a block of ice. What hurts me most is that she's been ordered to act in this fashion."

"Why don't you try to approach her in some other way, or invite her home?" I heard myself asking, wistfully.

Astrid curled up her lip in a sour grin, by which I gathered that she preferred to drop the subject altogether.

I was mistaken. She shrugged her shoulders, suggesting that at this stage I might as well hear the rest of the story.

"They got suspicious at the embassy and discreetly advised your father to persuade me to stop seeing Natasha alone. I must not interfere with his business or endanger his position vis-à-vis the government! Can you believe it, Alexis? My God, this Independence fever has got to him to the point where he even reminds me of my origins—something he always delicately avoided in the past. Does he forget that Jews don't fare too well with the communists—and not only with them!"

Strangely enough, as much as I felt outraged at the harm inflicted upon Astrid, and although I despised him for it, I couldn't ignore the fact that Orlando Romani was merely trying to save himself from the current tidal waves. It seemed that in those post-colonial times people were being screened and tossed about in a sort of purgatory. There developed a strong sense of solidarity among the various national groups which I found somewhat distressing. In the past, we were all like members of a single family, overextended perhaps, loosely knitted no doubt, but a family nonetheless, with its social distinctions and peculiarities, its loves and hates, and the inevitable gossip who fill in the gaps between the richer members and their less fortunate cousins. But now the movie theaters in the Asian quarter gradually ceased to be frequented by non-Asians. Europeans would no longer take their cars outside the city limits for their Sunday picnics. Hutus would avoid the company of their former Belgian or Arab friends for fear of being exposed. In a society from which politics had been as remote as the moon, everything now had a political tinge. And to appear less conspicuous, the town's 'prominentsia'—a lax term encompassing government figures, diplomats, foreign technicians, old time socialites and any 'decent' folk clean of conspiratorial stigmas—would regularly show themselves in such informal gathering places as the Club Nautique, the outdoor cafés of the three major hotels, and the twin cinemas bordering Independence Square. In this atmosphere of 'regained identities', Astrid felt at once betrayed and involved, against her will. "Your father has lost all his pride, if he ever had any," she continued, "he plays the ostrich when one of those newly appointed ministers makes a pass at me. 'Darling, you can't refuse him a dance, he'd be offended. Why are you so susceptible?' Easy justification! He might just as well throw me into the arms of anyone he owes a favor to. Am I not a *métisse*, the offspring of sin, a *batârde*!"

The words sounded so crude in her mouth, so ugly in their implication, that instead of showing compassion I choked in anger. Then I caught myself hollering something to the effect that if she considered herself so

low, was I not the scum of humanity since she and my
father had had the whimsical idea of falling in love with
each other? Couldn't they have chosen partners of their
own background and thus have avoided making a mess
of three lives? I went on and on, spewing out remarks
which baffled me, for what I was saying contradicted
everything I had so far believed in, that very sense of
dignity Astrid had so often spoken of. She raised her
eyebrows and gave me a startled look. For a moment the
diaphanous veins of her cheeks seemed to be splitting
like the tiny crevices of a damaged porcelain cup. A
silence ensued, an intolerable one such as happens
between two beings who after years of separation no
longer know what to expect of each other, a silence
during which, staring at the now blurred contours of
Astrid's face, I caught an image I wished would never
alter. Youth eternal, at its frailest.

"I'm sorry," she whispered, "it may not be proper
to say so, but you're the only one left who can take my
nonsense." And she chuckled.

I went to her, leaned against the armrest and brushed
her cheek with the back of my hand as if to make sure
it hadn't lost its velvety touch.

"You're wrong," I said, "he doesn't love you, he
idolizes you."

"I know," she smiled, "that's what's so sad, and
that's why we never could be friends. But don't worry,

Alexis, I haven't changed. Storms are bound to break occasionally, aren't they?"

"Last night you were dreaming out loud," Serena tells me while dipping a piece of toast into the yolk of her soft-boiled egg. "You were angry and kept repeating the name Natasha. A past sweetheart of yours?"

"She might have been," I sniggered, "but I was too young. Seriously, she was someone very dear to Astrid. In fact, the only person Astrid ever trusted, even though their relationship lasted such a short time. My mother, you see, did not like men. Or, at least, I think she was afraid of them."

"Oh!" Serena sighed, cupping her hand around her breast.

"What's the matter? Do you have a cramp?"

"It'll pass."

Her face turned livid. I gestured towards the door.

"Let's ask Mrs. Lindner for some more hot tea."

"Don't, it's all right, I assure you!" Serena insists, stretching her lips into a forced smile. Then with a tremor in her voice she inquires:

"But why didn't you tell me before?"

"What do you mean?"

"About your mother being afraid of men!"

All of a sudden I drop both of my elbows on the table and snap:

"Look here, if you're trying that Oedipus bit on me, you've got the wrong party. By now you should have understood that this is not the kind of thing I am worried about. And you know it damn well. What's come over you?"

She stares at me with her big piercing eyes and I can't figure out whether they are under a spell or ready to spurt out venom. Fear or hatred? I sense that my anger is misdirected, but there's a stubbornness in me which commands: "Don't give in, let her stoop for once."

Without so much as flinching, enigmatic in her stare, making me feel like little more than a shop window mannequin, she finally says:

"You're so self-centered, it's unbelievable. Didn't it occur to you that I might have been referring to someone other than Alexis Romani!" Then, exasperated by my dazed expression she continues:

"There are many Astrids in this world craving for the type of love only Natashas are capable of offering. Whether they can be fulfilled depends on a number of factors. The Orlando blindness being one of them, and not the least . . ." She goes on in a single fiery thrust, but I have ceased to listen, only now and then intercepting a harsh consonant or the recurring 'you' which bounces back at me with head-splitting effect.

I grab her wrists and squeeze them till she is forced to quiet down. Although it still isn't clear in my mind what Serena is trying to convey, I've at least acquired one certainty: in an odd fashion she wants me to identify her with Astrid. After all, it was the allusion to Natasha that set off her tirade. Smouldering Serena; a reluctant tear at the corner of her eye. I release the grip on her wrists and suggest, casting aside my so-called selfishness, that we should spend the afternoon talking: "Because I sense there are things you wanted me to hear long ago."

Having walked for about half an hour through the barren outskirts of Ashkelon and exchanged a few comments on today's bombing of a Jerusalem supermarket, we lazily settle on the lawns of the Antiquities Park, facing a cistern. From this angle, the sight we behold—dolmen-like structures interspersed among lush green foliage—has an eeriness at once pristine and so far removed from our immediate reality that I find myself being slowly drawn into a mood resembling a cataleptic trance. And whatever I hear or might say inevitably becomes shrouded in that aura, seeping into the mind as if through an opaque screen. The crimson smear of lipstick on her teeth lends her a virginal quality. They scintillate with the quivering of her lips. Crimson on ivory—a fortuitous, delectable combination. As she talks her breath exhales whiffs of eaten-up lipstick. She's blowing invisible particles of petals. Petals that have macerated for years, yet strangely retained their fragrance.

I learn that Serena is not sure what it means to love a man. And she isn't saying this because of my state of 'confusion'. In fact, Jerry is the only boy she has known before me. True, he had deflowered her, but it was more an act of friendship than love. She thought he had 'cured' her.

"Of what?" I ask.

The attraction she's always felt towards women, a sentiment she's kept from me for too long, much too long. And she's sorry for having lied. Though it's not really a lie, since she was convinced that one day she'd be rid of the ambivalent feeling.

"Haven't we spent years of relative happiness, before you got ill?" she asked. "We've always behaved independently, you, Alexis, frequenting your painter friends, and I seeing Diana or Carmen. You liked them too, didn't you? Well, I needed the one and the other, as much as I needed you, for reasons I hoped I never would have to explain. Until Jerry reappeared in my life—last month. He was aware of how I felt, and he wanted to marry me. I was distrustful, believing he was acting out of pity. That's when I decided I should leave the States. He somehow represented the cord I had to sever. We did correspond for a while. He was extremely hurt but eventually resigned himself to my decision. And here we are. Part of the Serena mystery has been unravelled."

And here we are, lying on the grass behind a tombstone, surrounded by tall poplar trees. Eons of solitude . . . and that mane shimmering in the dusk like a swarm of fireflies. Could Astrid have gone through a similar ordeal? Will I ever know? Dr. Bern, how the hell did I get to you? Where were my eyes? How much less painful it is to suffer in the same, overflowing stream than in those parallel counter currents!

"Go without me Alexis, I need some rest."

She has circles under her eyes. They're dim and shaped like almonds, almost pleasant to look at, like the powdered half-moons of the early movie stars.

l had an agitated sleep last night. Serena must have been still as a mummy for if she'd moved I'd have noticed it and gotten up.

As I'm about to suggest that we catch the noon bus, Mrs. Lindner brings us a plate of toast with strawberry jam.

"You know," she announces while clearing the rest of the table, "destiny plays very strange tricks. My psychologist nephew who works at Tel Ashomer Hospital, the one who gave you Dr. Bern's address . . . well, he wants to leave his wife. Let me first take this to the kitchen and I'll tell you all about it. *Mein Gott!*"

A minute later she's sitting with us, shaking her head:

"*Mein Gott*, such a brilliant boy! Two wonderful children and a wife who couldn't be more gentle. He's lost his head for some other woman. Must be. All of a sudden he finds Myriam old-fashioned. How about that!" Dear Grandma Lindner, her voice quivers with emotion and seems to drag its whole weight down her double chin. So soft and plump, it whets your appetite, an appetite for tenderness. And even when it wobbles furiously the way it does now, you can't help but want to be protective.

"He has the nerve to say that Myriam will in time adjust to the situation, and that since she is a good nurse, he will look to it that she gets a promotion. *Mein Gott*! What kind of talk is this! Changing a wife like you change a car. After eleven years together. Where has he put all that psychology of his? Actually, I've always been a bit sceptical about the type of people he goes around with. They're mostly psychiatrists. He even introduced me to a child analyst once. Imagine! Ah, ah, this constant delving into the mind is not healthy."

Then, as if excusing herself for neglecting me, she adds: "You did well, Mr. Alexis, to stop seeing that doctor, you don't need him, especially with this lovely girl by your side."

She pats Serena's shoulder in a gesture that is more an attempt of self-conviction than encouragement. But soon enough she reverts back to her initial story, sighing intermittently:

"I'll tell you what's wrong with many young folks today. Sure they have solid qualities. Without their courage, their devotion, Israel would be in an even worse state. It's that—what you call it—promiscuity, or whatever. They go from one girl to another, and vice versa, whether they're married or not. There's no sense of shame anymore. Just go to the beach. The other day I saw two men kissing in broad daylight, in front of everybody. They looked Scandinavian. But now this happens here too among our own youngsters. *Ach!*"

Now she pats my forearm: "You have a treasure. Cherish it. Look at me, I'm a widow, and I've had some good propositions. But in my heart no one could ever replace Joshua. May his soul rest in peace. Why is it so difficult to remain faithful nowadays? Must be the television, those movies where they try all sorts of funny things. When I went to see *Last Tango in Paris* I thought it would be a romantic film. What scenes, *mein Gott!* How can even actors lower themselves to such a point! I used to like that Marlon Brando. Maybe I don't understand this new generation. Who am I to criticize? But that nephew of mine, tsss, tsss!"

Another long-drawn sigh before she takes leave of us.

When we're alone, Serena muses, punctuating Mrs. Lindner's trend of thought: "We've become too complex."

# CHAPTER SEVEN

Independence Day in Tel Aviv. The air is brisk and translucent. The ground is strewn with leaves, hecatomb of last night's gale. A maze of bookstalls unfolded in this square not long ago. Municipal workers are now giving it the last touch, tying garlands of bright bulbs and star-spangled festoons between the lamp poles as a flag clatters intermittently against the awakening sky. In a few hours, the crowds will be spilling over like breakers and I shall be feeling claustrophobic. Around eleven, Serena will join me at the corner café where Jerry, Dave and Shoshana are going to be meeting us. The place is empty, yet I do not have that gripping sense of helplessness which stirred me the rare times I stood in front of Milan's desolate and awesome Duomo (cathedral). Here nothing really belongs to you, not even in fantasy. I've contemplated the Dead Sea scrolls in Jerusalem, shut my eyes but couldn't escape its haunting aura. The more I find myself sliding into the paradoxical realities of this land the clearer it becomes that I am—and surely not only I—a fractured part of its collective soul. Then will the individual in us cease to

clash with our social double? Or perhaps the meaning
of life is all contained in this paradox: striving toward
the irreconcilable. Isn't every glimmer of hope a step
towards eternity?

Young soldiers are beaming with pride, holding
their Uzi guns as naturally as if their weapons were
grafted to their sides. They could be Boy Scouts
displaying dangerous toys, or demons in the guise
of handsome ephebi. The hum of voices building up
among the crowd is at once indistinct and boisterous,
like waves unfurling. You can hear hearts pounding and
blood vessels throbbing in an orgasmic agony which
confounds the mind. The military parade goes on, tanks
crawling in pairs like prehistoric amphibians, followed
by trucks loaded with air-to-air missiles and the latest
pieces of weaponry. And just to remind us that we were
preceded by winged intelligence, jet formations perform
above us in bold aerobatics. Whistles of admiration
crackle around me. After a while, all I perceive is a
deep, muffled sound. There's a pungent quality in the
atmosphere caused by the heat mixed with the slightly
nauseating body exhalations. I suddenly feel as though
I'm trapped in the midst of a swarm of insects. A
nation of insects? Tons of defoliants dropped over the
European continent, wiping out huge populations, yet
unable to eradicate the entire species. Fleeing swarms

already darken the North American skies, reaching the far corners of our universe. Others, guided by a stronger instinct are hovering above these shores, upsetting a breed of long forgotten cousins. Having developed a surprising resilience to certain chemicals this particular breed takes over. The situation has reversed itself drastically. They're a destructive species. Are we so terribly different from these new insects? Mistaking our own shadows for the enemy?

We've been invited for evening snacks at Rebecca's, Shoshana's cousin. Jerry left us at the doorstep, excusing himself in a tone of unveiled disgruntlement. My guess is that the parade has disturbed him, and that he deemed it more honest to part company than hurt his hosts with upsetting remarks. Serena is boiling with anger. She didn't expect Jerry to let her down at the last minute.

We're introduced to Peter, a middle-aged German— though he looks no older than his late forties—, with grayish blue eyes and salt-and-pepper hair, whose ivory streaks hint that he might have been a pure blond in his youth. He's rather slender, even gaunt, and his face is sunburned. In spite of this healthy sheen, he doesn't look quite at ease among these people. But the moment he tells us that he teaches Italian literature at the University of Heidelberg I bombard him with questions in my native tongue, and he just as suddenly lightens up.

My wife appears indifferent to our conversation and sips at her glass of gin, as if she were daydreaming. I still want to make sure and whisper:

"Not very wise to drink on an empty stomach, is it!"

She looks up, frowns, and half-opens her mouth but then tells me with a swift tilt of the head to mind my own business.

Dave has noticed and throws in jovially:

"Wouldn't you like to listen to some nice music? Come on Rebecca, let's hear that Peruvian record you played a while ago. With those fantastic flutes."

Against the unadorned peach-colored wall facing me, the hanging shrub projects a spider-like shadow. The room looks larger than it actually is. In the middle stands a copper tray and all around it the floor is strewn with hand-woven rugs. Each of us has two or three cushions to lean on. Shoshana holds one that is quilted with splinters of mica. She cuddles it as though it were alive. There is a link between the flute's crystalline sound and Shoshana's oblong fingers so gingerly curved over the cushion. They're as enticing as her lips. I still want to wring that pathetically vulnerable neck of hers, like the time she sat in front of me the day we drove through the Negev desert.

A rustle of crinoline sweeps across the room, then reaches to the tray. It's Shoshana's cousin serving a plate of Oriental tidbits. She's shy to the point of appearing mute. Entirely dedicated to the goddess hospitality. In fact she's like a shadow and her role, delightfully old-fashioned, is to spoil her guests. She barely allows you to thank her before the embroidered babouches, laced around her feet, slip out of sight.

"This music makes me want to fly above our petty world. Like a condor. Serena, have you been to the Andes?" Dave asks, as if addressing the question to himself.

"A friend of mine . . . I mean of ours," Serena glances at me, creating a silence she already regrets, then she carries on, "Carmen, who's a painter, taught Indian children in a village near Lima before she finally decided to settle down in Milan."

"Why Milan?"

"Why not?" Serena retorts on the defensive, forcing me to intervene.

"Carmen's mother was Italian and wanted her to study at The Brera Art Academy."

"Let's talk about something else, will you?" Serena pleads; "sorry if I brought up the subject." I thought I was the one who needed help, or so I was led to believe. Now it is that American girl—my estranged wife—who worries me. Have our seven years together been a parenthesis? I'm slowly acquainting myself with a side of her she hoped would have faded away by now. She's like the statue I so often rush by in a side street of Piazza Scala, and whose features I stopped to notice only a couple of summers ago. From then on I've always given it, a wink however brief, as if it expected a sign from me. And whenever I look at its bronze eyes I have the feeling they are alive, still uncertain about my trustworthiness.

Serena's fingers tap nervously against the floor. Now and then the click of a nail breaks through the silence. I suddenly realize how hard and resistant nails can be. And galling! Yet when we sit together at home, holding hands, I instinctively pass my fingers over her slick nails, the same way you brush the black keys of a piano. I had that same feeling when my mother played a piece of Chopin on the baby grand in our sitting room in Africa. I would stare at her beautiful hands with admiration and imagined I could lick the polish off her fingernails. Now I wish Serena's were trimmed like a man's. Their sight irritates me and they no longer evoke that feminine touch which I secretly envied, on the contrary, I see claws ready to tear the skin. The tapping stops with the music.

She couldn't help it. Jerry should have stayed. Mrs. Lindner's nephew is leaving his wife. Why am I thinking of them? It's their problem. Was the military parade necessary? Dave and Shoshana took it for granted, or did they? And the thousands of spectators? Well, nobody in this country is really a spectator. The nation can't afford it. And Rebecca? In her quiet, submissive way, she too contributes to Israel's defense forces. A social worker:

the job suits her to a tee. Yet, I imagine her living in another epoch, doing chores in a humble household in some Russian shtetl during the reign of the czars. What has she gained with Israel's independence? Apart from the assurance that she will never have to suffer a pogrom? When she boards a bus, isn't there the risk that she might blow up in a suicide bomb attempt? And the two of us, what shall we find here that won't go to waste? What was our purpose in coming to this beautiful country, fraught with danger? Because this is indeed an amazing country, where half a century ago, except for the old quarters of Jerusalem and a few small towns, most of it was covered with brush and sand.

Serena is drowsy, whilst I'm livid. This time it is Shoshana who has taken the initiative of dissipating the tension that has built up around us; she suggests Peter recounts the incident he witnessed during the Second World War as a young boy and which has changed the course of his life. At first our German guest feels ill at ease and says that we wouldn't be really interested in this kind of a story, adding that we might even be a little shocked. But Dave and I insist and I revert to him in Italian. He lowers his gaze, pinching his lips in a sulky pout.

"Dai, Piero!" I say pleadingly, pressing my hand on his shoulder, as if we were long-time buddies.

"Ok, you've won, but on one condition, that you make no comment after I've finished my story."

That remark casts a sudden chill in the atmosphere, but Rebecca acts as if she hasn't heard it; she walks across the room and puts a new CD on the player. It is neither music nor the human voice, but echoes of nature, the flutter of wings, the splashing of waves, the rustle of a brook, or of leaves in the forest, sounds barely audible, so very soothing they seem to glide over your skin. We are suddenly immersed in a space full of magic.

Venice, 1984. Fleeting sentinels, a pair of seagulls glide past the stretch of milky sky whilst down in the campo two ragazzi play at calcio. "Goal" exclaims the eldest, prematurely, as he strikes the ball with all his might. "And missed again," counters a strident voice. Except for the two young boys, the square is desolate and the tall somber buildings huddling around it look on with their closed shutters, impervious to the scene.

1944. A small town in the Black Forest. Hans has, just turned 10.

I went to Onkel Ludwig's attic but found the door locked. Something was moving inside and I figured it must be a mouse. Then I heard a noise that sounded like somebody breathing. I looked through the keyhole and gasped. There was a girl sitting on the plank-bed. I could only see her face and the collar of her blouse. She had very black hair, cut like that of a page, and huge beautiful eyes, but with such sadness in them.

I stayed awake most of the night trying to figure out who she might be. A distant relative? No one in the family had black hair, dark brown yes, but not black. I don't know whether I was already dreaming but the girl kept begging me, "let me out, let me out." It can't be true. Onkel Ludwig is too gentle a man to want to harm a child. But then why is she locked up?

1984. Every stone in this city speaks to my heart as if I'd lived here for centuries. I feel as Venetian as these two young lads playing *calcio*. Yet, will I ever be able to cross the threshold of that Rest Home?

1944. I climbed the stairs ever so softly and pressed my eye against the keyhole. The girl was shaking her head in a pleading way. Then I recognized the large hand of Onkel Ludwig with the signet ring he wears on his little finger. "Mein Liebling," he whispered, stroking her cheek, "I won't hurt you." I became dizzy all of a sudden and then I got terribly scared and I ran outside.

1984. My God, to be so near. But here comes a party of tourists. The visit starts in about fifteen minutes. So few people ever get to see the place. It disturbs their tranquillity. There are only five of them.

"May I join you?" I ask.

The bearded young man with the rucksack answers almost jovially, "Please do."

One of the middle-aged ladies, a Canadian, having detected my accent, addresses me in Yiddish. She turns livid as soon as she realizes her mistake. In her look I read fear, fear mixed with anger and hatred. I want to shout it so loud the booming of my voice would shatter all the windows of the *campo*, "I'm sorry, sorry six million times . . . I was but a teenager."

Henceforth the Canadian lady won't say another word to me.

1944. Onkel Ludwig notices how agitated I am. "What is it, Hanslein?" he says with his kind frown.

I'm choking and the only gesture I'm capable of is point at the attic. The long, interminable silence that follows is suffocating like a thousand blazing tongues licking my face.

He puts his arm around my shoulders.

"It's a secret, Hanslein," he says at last, in a voice that seems to be someone else's. "You'll be the only one to know."

Before he goes on, as if taking my cue from him, I hear myself mumble: "I swear on Mutti's life I shan't repeat it, not even to her."

Onkel Ludwig kisses the top of my head then leads me to the attic. He takes a key out of the breast pocket of his uniform jacket and unlocks the door. Standing next to the plank-bed the girl stares at me with amazement, her long eyelashes blinking like a doll's. She's a little taller than me and wears boys' clothes. It's only when Onkel Ludwig introduces us that I learn that she is a he. I'm dumbfounded. What a princely looking . . . boy!

"Aldo will remain with me until the war is over," Onkel Ludwig explains, "he is in great danger, that is why I've taken him under my protection." He then says something to the boy in broken Italian and we part.

1984. Showing us into the German synagogue which houses the museum, our pretty guide gives us a brief history of the ghetto. She tells us that the word ghetto has its origins right here and is derived from *gettare*, for this used to be the site of a foundry in which projectiles were cast.

"Until the sixteenth century Venetian Jews lived scattered all over the city. Then an edict confined them to the *Sestiere di Canareggio* where we now stand, so that the authorities could keep them under close scrutiny. This is why the buildings here are among the tallest in the city. As many as 5,000 Jews resided in this area. To identify themselves, those working outside the ghetto had to wear a yellow hat. In spite of the constraints and uncountable vexations, the community managed to prosper and to establish in the Canareggio one of Europe's most flourishing centers of Jewish learning. They were so heavily taxed, however, that they gradually left Venice, and by the time Napoleon conquered the city—he was responsible for breaking down the ghetto gates and for granting equal rights to the Jews—the community numbered some one thousand inhabitants."

"And now?" asks the Canadian lady, "how many are there?"

"Much, much less, Madam," the guide says, adding, "I myself am a Catholic."

This is the only other moment the Canadian lady turns around to face me and her glare pierces my whole being.

1944. I'm burning to see Aldo again and await impatiently in Onkel Ludwig's lounge. He promised he'd be back around six this evening. It's already ten past the hour. I've always felt *gemütlich* in this cottage, maybe that's the reason I'm pushing aside the evil thoughts that keep sneaking into my mind during my sleep. But why should Aldo be in danger? Aren't the Italians our allies? I'm sure Aldo and I will become friends: I saw it in his eyes when I greeted him goodbye.

Really, Onkel Ludwig, what are you doing? It's a quarter to seven. I'll go and have a look upstairs.

My God! The door of the attic is open and Aldo has gone. There's a note on the plank-bed, it's for me.

"Hanslein, I've been called to the Front and I shall have to stay away for quite a while. Don't worry about our little mascot, I'm taking care of him. I'll write to you as soon as possible. Remember, though, the promise you made. I know I can trust my beloved nephew. Your Onkel Ludwig."

1984. "Of the five schole or synagogues in the *campo* only one is used for prayers," the guide informs us. We visit the Spanish and Levantine *schole* which have been restored to their original splendor.

"With its wood panelling, plaster decorations and gilt ornaments, the latter is a perfect example of Baroque architecture."

The guide also tells us that the Committee for the Safeguard of Venice has awarded its 1983 prize to the Jewish Community for its exceptional contribution to the restoration of the *schole* and of the Old Hospital which has been converted into a rest home for the elderly. The Rest Home . . . that's where she is.

1944. It's four months since Onkel Ludwig and Aldo left. And still no news. Mutti gave me the keys to the cottage—she keeps them during Onkel Ludwig's absence. Of course, Mutti doesn't know about Aldo.

Opening the lid of the plank-bed in the attic this morning I found, amongst my toys, my very first drawing pad—I was still in kindergarten. I turned the pages and what did I discover? A letter by Aldo in pencil, very tightly written. It's in Italian, of course, so I can't understand it. But on the bottom of the page there's an address in Venice with his full name: Aldo Levi.

1984. The visit comes to a close and we bid each other farewell. The two lads are no longer playing soccer. The *campo* is filled with ghosts, peaceful ghosts but also those that have returned from their forced exile. I walk over to the bas-relief commemorating the Holocaust. It is large and bleak and chills the spine. This is where the ghosts of the persecuted congregate. I can feel them in my bones. The question which will forever remain unanswered harks back, "How could my people, that highly civilized people who gave the world Beethoven and Goethe and yes, Karl Marx, commit the abomination of all time? How could we, Christians, suffer from such collective amnesia, forgetting that our own God was a Jew, that Mary and Joseph, his parents, were Jews? INRI. I'd better go back to the *pensione*. This place is driving me mad.

1945. The war is over. Onkel Ludwig's cottage has been destroyed during the last air raid. He will never come back to us. Mutti and I have cried a lot. Onkel Ludwig was such a good man. What has happened to Aldo? It is strange but I mourn for him alone, as if he were a brother, and every morning when I get up I have this ache in my chest. Yet I still pray the Lord in the hope that he may have been spared. Maybe he was lucky and is back in Venice with his parents. Oh, how I'd like to see him again! If only I could speak to Mutti about Aldo. I'd feel less pain. But no, I must remain loyal to Onkel Ludwig. I've hidden my drawing-pad with Aldo's letter. When I go to the Gymnasium I will learn Italian.

1955. Bonn. The months of research, the paper work, all that red tape! I thought I'd never see the end of it. The Ministry has finally released some information concerning Aldo's family. It's meager, but it's more than I had hoped for.

A couple of years ago a Franca Levi applied to the Ministry for war reparations. She is the sole survivor of a family of four. Her husband Davide and both their children Aldo and Liliana perished in Germany. Franca Levi couldn't afford to maintain their home, so she had to move to a much smaller place. Even with the allowance she now receives she has to do odd jobs to make ends meet. In the evening and on weekends she works as a seamstress.

Aldo is my obsession, my whole life revolves around him. Our all too brief encounter was enough to determine the course of my existence. Why else would I have taken up history and comparative religion and study Italian?

Aldo, angel-prince. To think that I could have once loved Onkel Ludwig makes me shudder. He saved you temporarily from their claws in order to better use you and satisfy his base instincts. How futile is my revolt!

1984. The pomp and the glory of Sunday mass at San Marco. You might have stood next to me right now if . . . if . . . and we certainly would have never met. Listen to the seraphic voices. Aren't these rituals mankind's most magnificent tribute to their creator? I have lost faith in Him, Aldo, the moment I set eyes on you.

1958. Bonn. Now that I hold a professorship at Heidelberg University and even though my stipend is still modest, I've arranged with the Ministry that part of it be added on a regular basis to the allowance it sends Franca Levi—with the provision that my contribution remains anonymous.

1984. Waiting at the entrance of the Rest Home. I've waited forty years for this moment. In my perfect Italian, concealing any trace of emotions, I shall tell her, "Signora Levi, you probably won't remember me, I used to live in the *Sestiere di Dorsoduro* behind the *Campo della Carità*. I was a friend of Aldo's and . . ."

Around me I can almost hear the collective beating of hearts, interspersed with sighs. Some irises are shining, others are unmistakably damp, but no one utters a word. The promise has been kept. Peter's visage is drawn, he is short of breath, as if he'd just been subjected to a session of exorcism. He wipes the sweat off his forehead, dabbing it with a checkered handkerchief, his hand trembles, yet he gives no excuse for the state he is in. Despite all the wrinkles, I can picture him as a young man; there is still something boyish and naive about his expression, contrary to most adults where the years of suffering are imprinted in their features, like brittle old shells swept by an umpteenth ocean wave.

Without having been asked, Shoshana puts on Yemenite music and starts dancing, languorously at first—her muscles are as fluid as those of a panther— then, without transition, and as if triggered by some internal mechanism, she starts undulating like a snake; as the beat of the tambourine picks up into a steady rumble, her naked feet hit the ground with increased frenzy. Her whole body seems absorbed in that swaying movement that is halfway between feline and reptilian; at a certain point she appears to be shivering, from her toes to the root of her hair, like a bee hovering above the corolla of a flower, ready to gather its pollen. Her mimetic capabilities are quite extraordinary. She must have had several lives, and impersonated a variety of animals; at times, simultaneously. She concludes her fascinating show with a belly dance, which is punctuated by whistles and the ever louder clapping of hands. Shoshana is now definitely in a trance, her eyes rolling upwards, whirling on her toes, in the manner of an Ottoman dervish. Her gestures, so typically oriental, are bewitching. The scene is unreal and yet she makes it appear so natural; and then we're suddenly thrust into the middle of a film sequence unfurling in slow motion: she glides to the floor and her body embraces it like a pool of lava that has finally settled. Her cheek hugs a polished slab, her arms join above her head to form a crown.

This evening has been so emotionally charged that I feel a pain in my chest, my eyes prickle but remain terribly dry, as if the tears had been swept away by a *hamsin* wind. Every conscious minute spent in this country seems to snatch out yet another layer of serenity, or whatever resembled that happiness I shared with my wife in Milan. Was it all an illusion? Or have I been contaminated by some of my tourist peers who suffer from the Jerusalem syndrome? It may be so, yet, when I find myself in Israel's capital city, the omnipresence of religion, whether Jewish, Christian or Moslem, nauseates me to the point where, with each new step, I have the impression of sinking into a quicksand, whereas my lungs get filled with the toxic fumes of prayers. This fabled and tortured city, whose pink and violet twilights are a painter's dream, proves untameable, she is too much for me, even though I yearn to be treated with humanity, offering her in return my sincere and truthful compassion.

Yes, I loathe religion which is institutionalized, the arrogance of dogma, its indecency. That monster of hypocrisy encompasses every ingredient that leads to violence and child pornography. Ah that prurient need which men have to plead God in public! Just look at them in St. Peter's Square or around the Kaaba in Mecca. Those millions of lost souls who believe faith will come back to them through the booming echoes of their peers. What more resounding proof of inner weakness and lack of personality! They scream in unison, to better blend themselves into the sea of human solitude. And in some cases that blind obsession of God gives way to a culture of hatred and death of which today's Islamists are the most lurid bearers.

I came to sit next to Peter, who now appears more relaxed. We chat in Italian and discover that we have several points of interest in common. He is the one suggesting that we should see each other again. I accept at once, but with mixed feelings. Of joy, first, because it has been such a long time since I could focus on something other than my existential problems, here was someone I could talk to, without having the impression of demeaning myself, and what's more, like me, he's an outsider—I wouldn't say 'foreigner' in my case: even if I didn't want to admit it before, there's an indestructible if not fuzzy bond that ties me to this land. Then there's the apprehension of latching onto a new relationship, for the scars inside are still very raw and the slightest rub of emotion, be it of benevolence, would reopen the wound. Unfortunately I have never really mastered the art of diplomacy, in spite of all those years spent at KBI, even less that of concealment. They should maybe isolate me lest I contaminate my peers, but more so, to protect myself from being hurt.

Yet, I feel strangely attracted to this man whose perfume I recognize and which brings me back to my childhood in Rwanda-Urundi—Father used to sprinkle his face with it every morning—and to the summer vacations I spent with the family years later, on the Italian Riviera.

"Am I wrong or are you wearing 4711 eau de cologne?" I ask him with faint nonchalance.

"Indeed," he answers, staring at me wide-eyed, "you have a fine nose, inasmuch as it is quite difficult to find, outside of Germany. It used to be very popular when I was a young man, I suppose it is considered outmoded nowadays, but I still cling to it."

To allay the mawkishness that is taking over me, I suddenly change subject and inquire about his courses at the university. Does he still like teaching? How different is the student mentality now from what it used to be when he started his career? I listen to him with strained attention, albeit sympathetically.

Serena beckons at me: we have to go. Peter and I exchange addresses. This week he is staying in Tel Aviv and invites me to spend a day with him in the Mediterranean metropolis, along with my wife. I tell him, lowering the tone of my voice, that I would rather see him alone, and we set a date for the following Thursday at his hotel. I catch a glimmer of satisfaction in his eyes. He probably thinks, as I do, that a third person would make it more difficult for us to become acquainted more intimately. We are really on the same wavelength, he and I. The way he winks at me confirms it.

# CHAPTER EIGHT

A little surprised at first that I should want to go alone to Tel Aviv, Serena acquiesces, insisting however that I travel on a *sherut* and not by bus, on account of the terror attacks.

Towards the end of the ride my heart started to pound like mad and I was sweating profusely.

"Stop this nonsense!" I scolded myself, "you're not running to a date." But then I thought, "What am I getting into? I've just met this guy; true, he looks like a gentle and understanding person, but he's only an acquaintance. Don't expect anything more, or you'll burn your wings."

Yet, the moment I meet with Peter in the lobby of his hotel, a modest but pleasant enough place located two streets away from the waterfront, my tongue begins to twist. It sounds as if the words spilling out of my mouth end up in a mushy garble.

He probably accounts that to a certain shyness on my part and greets me with a wide, almost affectionate smile, pumping my hand vigorously.

"I've learned to love this city, beyond its commercial and trendy façade," he says. "In spite of it being relatively young in age—before 1909, there was nothing but sand and brush here—it harbors a remarkable number of treasures; with a bit of patience and a curious mind, you will discover them, like those Bauhaus and Art Déco buildings which are scattered all over the city. Do you know what Tel Aviv stands for, in Hebrew? 'Hill of Spring'. And that it is a trove for architects worldwide? Not to mention all the museums—the one on the Jewish diaspora is exceptional—the painting galleries, the arts and crafts boutiques, be they traditional, oriental or contemporary, whether you're looking for original and striking jewels or for the latest Israeli fashion in clothing.

The spur of enthusiasm on his part surprises me, for I remember how poised and discreet he was the other evening at Shoshana's, and even a little glum, when he was asked to recount that painful period of his childhood during the war.

"Would you like me to be your guide around the city?" He goes on; his eyes sparkling.

His joyous mood is contagious and I accept his offer gladly. It's so very unexpected; how relieved I suddenly feel that someone else is taking over, after all those weeks spent in negative brooding, fighting within myself, it's as if the compact mass of black clouds in my head has been swept away by a stream of crisp air. I ought to be watchful though, lest this invigorating breeze evolves into a whirlwind, not so much on account of Peter, of whose life I really know so little, rather because I still don't trust my own reactions.

There is something unreal about this whole thing and a myriad of images jostles through my mind as between the vacillating lines of a mirage, inasmuch as the temperature had already risen to a peak of 30 degrees celsius at eleven this morning.

We stroll along the boardwalk, dominating the wide stretch of golden sand, scattered with breakwaters that set off the limits to a succession of beaches, each portion having its particular character, with here, a palette of half naked bodies, soaking up the sun—healthy looking young guys and girls, many of them having a day off from their military duties—next to the one occupied by a small crowd of gay jocks, sporting their well-oiled muscles, some wearing just a g-string, there, a patchwork of bikinis and one-piece swimsuits—this is the larger stretch, patronized by families and people of all ages—and a little further, a checkered pattern of fully-clad orthodox Jews, taking in the light sea air.

God—is it at all fortuitous to invoke Him, when in the Bible, sodomites are promised to burn in Hell?—what a difference with my last trip, five, or is it seven years ago, when homosexuals used to hug the walls not to attract attention. I hear that there was a Gay Pride parade in the city not long ago and that Jerusalem will have its own next year. At the other end, lies Kikar Atarim, with its string of swanking hotels, its marina, its swimming pools, its posh restaurants and gaudy ice-cream parlors. Then there's the continual bustle of Dizengoff Square, whatever the hour, and the flea markets, where East and West mingle, in a flurry of accents, in an orgy of colors and smells.

Peter also introduced me to the homes of the poet Bialik and of Ben Gourion, who announced to the world the creation of the State of Israel. We then visited the Helena Rubinstein Pavillion, Jacob's Garden, with its rockery and flowerbeds, the Bible House, the Alphabet Museum and the Kings of Israel Square, where people flock by the thousands during political gatherings, or else to celebrate the victories of the Maccabi soccer team. In spite of the sweltering summer heat, this city never rests. Its exuberant and motley youth seems to be caught in a perpetual merry-go-round, and, contrary to the opinion that some people overseas have about the Israelis' supposed racism, I have never seen such a concentration of mixed couples and such a rainbow of skin hues, not to mention that nowhere on this planet, save perhaps in New York City, are you thrust into a similar Babel of languages. So much for clichés.

By road, Jerusalem is a mere 60 kilometers away, however, the mental distance that separates these two metropolises is enormous, and even though the young people of the capital dress like their peers in Tel Aviv, perhaps a little less flamboyantly, and share the same tastes for high technology, they are steeped in a pervasive atmosphere of religiosity, whether they're devout or not. The former set the tone, with a liberty that could, at times, appear insolent and overwhelming, whilst the latter try to be as discreet as possible, meshing into the crowds of the thrice holy city. It is therefore not surprising that these opposing mentalities sometimes clash.

We walk, leisurely, this time, through the half deserted rooms of the extraordinary Diaspora Museum, located inside the grounds of Tel Aviv University, and which recounts the 4000 year-old (according to the Hebrew calendar, we're in 5765—whatever happened to the difference of 1765 years?) history of the Jews, scattered at the four corners of the planet.

A welcome retreat, after all these often mind-boggling and always emotionally intense sights, is to sit at a terrace café overlooking the port of Jaffa, sipping a delicious papaya juice. The city, restored with a lot of taste, is now part of the Greater Tel Aviv municipality. It is, according to Peter, the oldest harbor in the world and it encloses within its thick stone walls antique shops, art studios and handicraft boutiques. From here, the big white metropolis appears, with its long stretches of beaches, like a fantastic vision. The smell of barbecued lamb and fried fish, wafting from the bistro next door, titillates my taste buds.

It's 7 pm. Peter suggests that we go back to Tel Aviv proper and have dinner together. I can always get a ride back to Ashkelon, he says, for there are *sheruts* until late at night. But before we go to his hotel, in order to refresh ourselves and rest a little, he offers to show me a last sight. A couple of streets away, stands the Shalom Tower, one of city's oldest, if not the oldest, skyscrapers.

I'm bewildered by my sudden surge of energy and ask myself how it was at all possible, in my present state, and with the debilitating heat surrounding us, that I could manage to visit all these places, for I don't even feel tired. It seems as though my body is split into two different, disconnected parts: whereas my clothes are soaked in perspiration, and I feel hot and sticky, my limbs appear to respond to some external power, over which my mind has no control.

We've reached the top of the Shalom Tower, which is the observation deck. Symphonies in blues and whites: the sea, the city and the sky, the air is crystalline, while the wind blows, mighty as the breath of a dragon. I want to scream, so overwhelming is the spectacle; my heart races at a maddening pace and, all at once, I wish the world would halt. Is it the beauty of what lies before me, its immensity, the frustration of not being a bird at this very instant, that I'm suddenly hyperventilating and feel so terribly constricted, a prisoner behind the fence that separates me from the precipice?

Leaving Peter to his momentary contemplation, I whisper "Wait for me here, I'll go all around the building."

I walk away from him, brush past several other tourists and locate a narrow space entrenched between two metallic columns. It is small but wide enough for a person of my build to climb over the guardrail and wedge himself sideways in it. I make sure no one comes near me, at least during the few seconds I need in order to hurl myself into the void. With a little effort, I am able to reach the guardrail, but as I am about to climb over it, the left side of my shorts gets hooked onto a sharp edge. Rage mixed with a growing sense of panic takes hold of me, and the more I try to wrench myself out of the nail-like object, the fiercer my shorts cling to it, in spite of its widening tear.

A woman's voice suddenly booms out: "Somebody, quick! There's a guy who wants to jump off."

Eyes half-closed, with fear now replaced by shame, I feel two strong arms clasp around my waist, forcing me to get down. It's the security guard I saw a little earlier. A revolver tucked in the holster clutched onto his belt, he looks at me with daggers in his eyes and, then, all the while he is tightening his grip around my fists, and hurting me with intent, he lets out a couple of Hebrew swear words: "*Balagan* (damn it!) . . . *Meshugga* (nuts)". In a louder and hoarser voice he adds, this time in English and rolling his r's in the guttural Israeli fashion: "Who do you think you are, James Bond? I have no time for such stupid games, ok!"

I'm red as a beet, for I sense that my Saviour despises me and is ready to spill out more abuse, but, alerted by the commotion caused by my failed suicide attempt, Peter rejoins me. He looks aghast and his hands begin to tremble.

The security guard beckons to him and asks: "Do you know him?"

"Yes . . . yes!" utters my companion.

"Do you want me to call Emergencies?" the guard bawls, "'cause this guy ought to be locked up."

Peter glances at me in search of some guidance. I stare back with imploring eyes, shaking my head like a mechanical puppet, at the end of its tether.

"We won't need it, thank you. I shall take care of him." he says. Then, recovering his composure, he takes me away energetically and asks in an improvised and scolding tone, aware that we are still very much the focus of attention, so as to put an end to the affair and clear the way: "Of course, you've forgotten to take your medicine again, huh. Worse than a child. Come on, let's go home."

When we reach the ground floor, stepping further down the street, Peter says, now almost in a whisper, midway between pity and sternness:

"In front of that security guard, I had to appear furious and patronizing, otherwise we would never have seen the end of it. Sorry about that."

Now that we're far from the scene, he pursues in a normal tone of voice, "I don't want to be inquisitive, but there must be a long history of pain and frustration behind that desperate gesture of yours. Feel free to open up, but only if you wish to. In the meantime, we both need to refresh ourselves, don't you agree?"

Ten minutes later, once we arrive in his hotel room, Peter asks whether I shouldn't call my wife, suggesting that she come to fetch me, for he isn't comfortable with the idea of me returning to Ashkelon alone.

"Oh no!" I exclaim, somewhat hysterically, "she mustn't know what has happened, at least not just now. In fact, it would be best if I didn't go back to Ashkelon this evening. To see her would only make things worse. I'll reserve a room in this hotel, if you don't mind."

Peter gives me a puzzled look, then says, after a short silence:

"If I heard the receptionist correctly this morning, they are expecting a group of Christian pilgrims today and consequently the place will be fully booked."

My companion frowns and purses his lips in a reflective pout.

"It has just crossed my mind: how about staying here with me tonight, the bed is wide enough for the two of us. That is if it's ok with you. I usually sleep like a log, so you won't disturb me at all."

My eyes tingle, just short of tears. For a second Peter remains agape, asking himself whether he hasn't blundered. But I reassure him:

"You've been so solicitous towards me, in spite of what you've just witnessed. How can I thank you?"

"Don't mention it," he says, on a more jovial tone, "I feel so clammy, I can't wait to go under the shower, and so do you, I'm sure. You really ought to call your wife though," he insists, "she'll get terribly worried. And since she's met me already, she won't think you were kidnapped." he concludes with a grin.

In response I smile, nodding my head.

"That's better!" says Peter, relieved, "Later on I shall take you to a little family bistro where you will be able to choose between Central European dishes and an excellent Moroccan couscous, the sole North African specialty of the house."

"I don't fancy Ashkenazi cuisine," I retort with a grimace, "especially gefilte fish, yuk, on the other hand, I love oriental food."

Back from the bathroom, hair still dripping, a towel tied round his waist, Peter says:

"Don't put your soiled clothes back on again, I'll lend you clean ones. I'm a little taller than you, but we have approximately the same build. I have a pair of Bermudas that are a little too short for me, but they should fit you perfectly."

Under the shower, I let the hot water run over my body until it gets almost burning; the initially pleasant sensation gives way to masochistic torture. It is a ritual I submit myself to regularly, not only in order to cleanse my body of the day's impurities, but as an exorcism from all the obsessive ills that have taken hold of me these last weeks. I feel dirty inside, as well as accursed. Then I open the other tap violently and the sudden stream of cold water paralyses me, to the point where, for a few seconds, I gasp for air. In going through these motions I have the feeling that the devil in me is momentarily shell-shocked and that, by the same token, all my sinister thoughts, like the one that triggered the incident at the Shalom Tower, are swept aside.

Water has decidedly magic qualities, even if they are ephemeral; would it be due to that supposed atavistic memory going back to the times that preceded the appearance of mankind on our planet, and of whose secrets the aquatic species are the sole guardians? It seems to me that a small number of human beings I have come across, more sensitive perhaps than the average man, or more superstitious, perceive the echo of this memory, be it in a distant or fuzzy way. I've noticed these traits among some people who are Pisceans like myself, though, regarding astrology, I am an agnostic of sorts, believing and, just as soon, not believing in it. Why should I otherwise feel so euphoric, not to say 'untouchable', the moment I immerse myself in seawater? Am I not, unconsciously, rejoining my prehistoric ancestors?

I find Peter in a drowsy state, lying bare-chested on the bed.

Wrapped up in his bathrobe and, my skin still tingling with goose pimples, I feel strangely invigorated. He opens his eyes and murmurs, half dazed:

"Sorry, but I did need to rest after this long, eventful day.

"Don't move," I tell him, as he is gesturing, about to rise, "I'll follow your example and stretch out too. It's still quite early, so then, as you said, we have the whole evening in front of us."

He closes his eyes and slips back into a slumber. For the first time since we've met, I can observe with ease that stranger whose goodness of heart I no longer doubt. I find him rather handsome, despite the years that separate us. Except for the light russet down inside his armpits and the narrow thread running along his belly, he is hairless, and since his skin is still taut, he doesn't look his age, inasmuch as he shows no sign of impending baldness. Having untied my bathrobe, I go and lie beside him, putting a comfortable distance between us. Never before have I been so intimately close to another man, sharing his bed, and what's more, naked. A sense of confusion takes hold of me and I begin to shiver once again, but not for the same reason this time, for suddenly I long to touch him. Initially it is a feeling of genuine affection, which, little by little, unobtrusively, evolves into a growing sexual desire. Then, before I can even evaluate the consequences of my boldness, I inch towards Peter's body, snuggle up against him and finally place my face on his chest. Startled, my companion raises his chin and gives me a quizzical look, yet the rest of his body remains still, as if by moving even slightly he might break the spell or drop a crystal vase standing on the rim of a pedestal table. After a short while, he lays his hand over my head. His fingers quiver, hesitating between caress and immobility. I've put him ill at ease, but this feeling vanishes as soon as I embrace him, squeezing his waist with my two arms forcefully, going so far as to sink my nails into his flesh. He utters a little cry and I burst out sobbing.

"Let loose, Alexis," he says, "you must feel totally free with me, I'm your friend."

These last words open the gates of my heart and I bury my forehead in the hollow of his shoulder. My sobbing gets louder and is interspersed with hiccups, but I soon become aware of the fact that our neighbors could hear me, especially since the walls of the room aren't very thick. I force myself to calm down.

Peter sits up and opens the drawer of the bedside table, retrieving a Kleenex, which he brings to my face, gently rubbing the tears around my eyes. I have stopped weeping. With a suddenness that baffles me, I press my mouth against that of my benefactor. His muscles stiffen yet he doesn't push me away. Emboldened by my impulsive gesture, I tighten my grip around Peter's chest and try to force my tongue against his teeth, hoping that he will let me in. He yields and we soon mix our saliva in a sequence of torrid kisses, skin against skin. I then unfold the towel from around his loins, and without waiting for his approval, climb over him, covering his body with mine. As our genitals rub against each other, causing us both to have an erection, a thought flashes through my mind and I realize at once that I'm having my very first homosexual experience, except for the fleeting incident which took place in the Negev desert with the young Palestinian.

In the past I have indeed fantasized making love to other men, but that always belonged to the register of some vague unattainable desire. I actually never pursued the thought and wasn't obsessed by it the way some closet homos, whether married or not, are, continuing to live locked within their own frustrations, either because of their Puritan upbringing or because of the social scandal which might ensue if they decided to reveal their true nature. I was raised a Catholic in the Belgian Congo, yet, in spite of it, I have never believed in original sin, nor in that of the so-called weak flesh, at least not after my adolescence, and whatever frustrations I had were more of an existential nature than sexual. In fact, what might seem strange, given my African origins and the rumors one hears about the precariousness of sexuality in the tropics, I had no inclinations whatsoever, one way or the other. In hindsight, I will go so far as to conclude that I was totally asexual, inasmuch as I have learned, only recently, that there exists indeed such human beings, men or women, young and old, who claim that they have absolutely no desire to have sex with anyone, be they of their own gender. Whereas my school pals broached the subject of girls with prurient fervor and often with vulgarity, as is so common with teenagers all over the world, I would listen to them without commitment, and, when forced to participate in their conversations, I would improvise an excuse and walk away.

I may be repeating myself, but only images moved me, such as reproductions of paintings of the Italian Renaissance or of the French Romantics and of statues of the Greek and Roman antiquity, which I would admire in the hefty gilt-lined art book my parents gave me for my thirteenth birthday. There was Venus and Adonis, Leda and the Swan, Apollo of the Belvedere, the countless pictures of Saint Sebastian who stirred such a strong fascination in me with all those arrows piercing his flesh and who exuded a mixture of pity and sensuality. I also remember Van Loo's marvellous portrayal of Diana and Endymion, along with the myriad of half naked heroes, painted with such lyricism and fortitude by Ingres or Jacques-Louis David. There was, in the vision of these hunky gods, of these luscious goddesses and of all the great historical characters involved, whether they were taken from the Bible or from other ancient civilizations, a quality so transcendental that their feats, however nefarious and unpredictable, and their often perverse love affairs, which would be subjected to public opprobrium if they were perpetrated by common mortals, somehow didn't offend me. These demigods, who were the apex of beauty, indulged in incest, paedophilia or even bestiality, without restraint or any sense of guilt. It is because of such an image, wherein the most elementary laws of morality could be infringed upon, often with impunity, that I could not, until my early adult years, associate carnal love with the people around me, and especially those of my age, for I would sublimate it. And since I only lost my virginity when I was twenty, seduced by a mature woman who could have been my mother, all other forms of love belonged, in my eyes, to the realm of abstraction, homosexuality being just another fantasy. Maybe the desire for the latter remained buried in my subconscious, this being said, I don't remember having suffered from the lack of it. My real attraction to men manifested itself quite late in life.

Peter's body arouses me as I never have been aroused in the past, even at the height of my love-making with Serena—our sex could be most gratifying, even though it always remained within the conventional bounds of matrimony, for I never pushed my curiosity elsewhere, nor have I ever suggested that we try a ménage à trois, or even partner swapping, for that matter.

The contact of this man's skin drives me wild: his musky fragrance, the slightly pungent whiff of 4711 eau de cologne, which he's just sprinkled himself with—the very same lotion my father used to put on in the tropical heat of Africa—makes me want to sink into his arms, and remain in this position forever. How long did that stretch of paradise last? I don't know, but the moment his hand brushes the curve of my hip I slowly come to, still impregnated with an intoxicating feeling of tenderness, and suddenly my blood whiplashes. With a renewed surge of vitality, I give him a hungry kiss, biting his lip so hard that, for a moment, I think he wants to recoil from me, but it is quite the opposite, his next gesture is one of possession. Then, discovering his cock for the first time in so splendid an erection, I stare at it, flabbergasted. It's so impressive, so unexpected, his balls are so perfectly round and firm, they remind me of a peach almost ripe, with its orangey-tan color, that seeing him so reserved and withdrawn in society, you would never suspect him to be such a passionate lover and even less to be so prodigiously endowed.

I don't have the time to dwell on these thoughts, for he now aims at my chest, licking it in small gulps the way a cat does with a bowl of milk. The moist contact of his tongue sets my skin ablaze, paralyzing me at the same time. As he begins to bite my nipple, the fire spreads around my loins, and my cock, which until now has remained gingerly half erect, blossoms to its full girth. It now appears that nothing can stop us and I spread my thighs as widely as I can so that he can take me unabashedly.

Seconds later, I feel his mouth cupping my glans then sliding up and down the shaft. I fight the urge to thrust my cock violently against the roof of his palate. He keeps on blowing me whilst at the same time his finger probes between my ass cheeks, he does it so gently, with such expertise, drawing light circles around my rosette, that

I begin to gulp for air. This is something new to me, it is a sensation which I've never felt or even fantasized about: another taboo has just fallen, for the thought of sodomy, a thought so fuzzy that it remained locked in the murkiest area of my mind, has always repelled me. His middle finger has now found its way into the most intimate part of my body as if it were the most natural gesture; it is soft and moist and I feel so aroused, sensing that I will come any moment, that I motion him to pull back. But instead, Peter firmly grabs my balls and I ejaculate inside his throat, in starts and fits, with spurts of come so abundant that I have the impression my bones are going to empty themselves of their marrow and that my bloodstream will dry up at the same time, whilst the spasm runs from the roots of my hair down to the soles of my feet, zigzagging through the myriad of nerve endings that form the planet of my being, for it is a planet indeed, of which I am suddenly conscious, across the misty valleys of pleasure.

A sudden flash of light explodes inside my head, but it feels strangely disconnected, as if it belonged to a stranger. I have tasted carnal bliss with Serena, more so than with any other woman, yet, what is happening to me now is not like anything I have known in the past. It is a revelation, a rebirth of sorts, like something new emerging from within my cells, which has remained dormant throughout all these years. I keep my eyes shut, lest that euphoric moment escapes me, even if my muscles have relaxed, while my body gently settles on the mossy bed of an enchanted no man's land where I hear rumors in the far distance that sound like the twittering of birds and the splashing of waves.

I don't remember having made the slightest move and yet here I find myself lying on my stomach. Would Peter, with that delicacy so typical of him, have gently pushed me over towards the middle of the bed, whilst my mind continued to float on top of a cloud? Slipping into that semi-conscious limbo that leads from drowsiness to the world of lusty dreams, I perceive a sudden shiver that soon whips my senses: something has insinuated itself along the crack of my buttocks, it feels like a cool breeze, unobtrusive at first, but then becomes very obvious and gets more and more playful. Two palms grab the fleshy globes of my ass then firmly part them open; before my brain can register what is going on, wrenching me out of my half-daze, a flush of hot breath sears through my hole, turning into irrepressible desire. It is so unexpected that I muffle a cry: is it surprise, shame, pleasure, or a combination of these three? It is no longer a finger that teases my opening but a tongue licking the most secret part of my body, which I had until now deemed to be the most execrated.

A friend in Milan had suggested that I read some of Sade's erotic works—'pornographic' is more appropriate here, even though no judgment is intended when using that word—and chancing upon the section in which the author graphically describes the practice of anal sex, I remember the utterly negative effect it had on my sex life for a long time after that discovery, so great was my aversion. Guido, a talented painter and a militant communist, was an inveterate womanizer, whilst he at the same time openly professed his bisexuality. He believed in Flower Power and in free casual sex. I think he was, in his ironic and jocular manner, somewhat infatuated with me and hinted more than once that I should try being buggered, that he would initiate me to such delicacies. I would reject his proposition in the same light tone, not showing, of course, my disgust. Half hiding his disappointment, he accused me, mockingly, of wanting to remain a prude.

"With that kind of petit-bourgeois attitude you will never be sexually liberated." He wasn't that wrong.

The way Peter licks my rosette, nibbling it as if it were a live mussel that he would savor with relish before swallowing it, drives me wild. Then suddenly, without warning, the tip of his now very stiff cock gags my hole. It's so moist it absorbs his glans in one gulp. But when the reality hits me, I feel my anus close in like the shell of an oyster and a searing pain shoots through my innards.

"Stop it!" I shout.

Frozen by fear, Peter complies, remaining in that position lest he should hurt me even further. An oppressive silence hovers above us, then my lover heaves a sigh, which is repeated in short bursts. He wants to back out, is he suddenly feeling guilty? For some reason I could not fathom right then, so unfocused were my thoughts and desires, that I caught myself mumbling, almost in a rasp:

"Please, stay the way you are."

Am I losing my mind? Anticipating a pain even sharper than the one I have just endured, and instead of shying away, I give a strong jolt, forcing him to penetrate me more deeply. It is I now who take the initiative and I begin to rock vigorously back and forth so that my lover's cock locks inside my sheath. I'm hallucinating, whilst my cheeks dribble with perspiration, to the point where images start floating around me, I keep banging and gyrating as if my very life were dependent on it. Yet, with infinite care, Peter slips in and out of my entrails, pausing every two or three seconds, making sure he never hurts me. I beckon then at once beg him to resume his motion, and I accelerate the pace, pumping against his midriff, faster and faster, with increased intensity and lustiness. The pleasure I now experience is inexpressible, and for the first time, I imagine what a woman feels when she yields to her man, after a terribly long wait.

Is this what is meant by losing one's virginity, is it tantamount to losing one's manliness? And suddenly the enormous hypocrisy that has been perpetuated through the ages within the different religions of man comes to my mind, that hypocrisy which still laces our planet like the myriad of stinging fibrils of a jellyfish.

In today's Western society where gays have earned a parcel of dignity and of freedom, a parcel, yes, since they still have to fight against kith and kin for mere acceptance, if not tolerance, the insulting words of 'fag', 'wimp', 'wuss', or 'sodomite', are still very much in use, whether in sportsmen's locker-rooms or in right-wing circles which continue to believe that homosexuals are sinners and deviants who remain a threat to family institutions. And I think of the prisons in Russia or even in France, at this very moment, where so many young inmates get raped by their elders and are treated like prostitutes who can be bullied and abused, as a way of venting their frustrations against society, infecting these poor guys with AIDS and other venereal diseases, without the guards taking any notice of such crimes. The ironic thing with such bullies is that, playing the active part, they bugger these youths without any remorse, claiming that they're not gay, oh no, certainly not, they just need a sexual outlet, it's the little pimps who are the friggin' fags. Then I ponder, asking myself whether the love between two men, or for that matter, between two women, isn't a form of narcissism, pushed to the extreme. One doesn't look any longer for a partner of the opposite sex, but for his or her own projection, in other words, for another image of the self in the mirror. Is that why homosexuals still bear the stigma of abnormality, unless they're considered inferior or simply unstable by many of their so-called peers? This is contradictory, inasmuch, as I do believe that we all are bisexual in nature, whether one admits it or not. Is it then so surprising that, in our liberated societies, more and more men, married men—who either continue to love their wives or feel estranged by them—avowed bisexuals, men who want to try 'something else, something new' to pepper their life, find solace and relief in all-male bath houses? Look at how men's fashion is increasingly influenced by the way gays dress or by how they take care of their bodies. Yet, the taboo of homosexuality persists and people who manage to cross the line often feel they have transgressed it, as if somehow they will bear the shame of their 'sin' forever. Of course, those who live among kindred spirits, or the big cities' more liberated youth, no longer feel shackled by centuries of opprobrium, some even dare to defy the politicians on their own turf, outing them for all to see, scoffing at the religious fundamentalists by loudly demonstrating during their extravagant Gay Prides.

But what are all these folks so afraid of? Of losing their virility, by merely frequenting gay people, or is it that they're afraid of heeding their instincts, or simply of wanting to have a taste of the forbidden fruit, prodded that they are by the most human of impulses, curiosity? When you know that in Yemen, among other Arab countries, that in northern Nigeria, the hateful sha'riah is applied, whereby homosexuals, caught in the act, are sentenced to death, and that those who are simply suspected of the 'abomination', get flogged in public squares then tortured and imprisoned, you wonder if Allah and his prophet recognize at all these perpetrators. The latter push the hypocrisy to the point of accusing them of a sin imported by the heathen West, as if homosexuality, which has always thrived in the Arab countries, was foreign to their patriarchal societies where the women are the most oppressed in the world. I doubt that the ayatollahs of all stripes—and here I include the Evangelical extremists, the Vatican censors, as well as the adepts of Meir Kahane—who regularly view pornographic films and videos to control what their flocks can or cannot see—never harbor any prurient and disavowable thoughts. The Church is often rocked by the revelation of paedophiliac scandals among their own preachers. And I then say to them: "Stop your shenanigans, stop aiming at the wrong targets and let consenting adults love whoever they want and in whatever manner they choose. It's none of your bloody business, if you wish to repress your own sexual instincts, that is your affair, not ours. Put your energy where it is needed, that is, with the poor, the suffering and the homeless, otherwise, go to hell and high water, which is what you promise with so much zeal those who according to you commit the sin of the flesh."

I realize how this kind of outburst may sound naive and even a bit ludicrous, but I won't apologize. To claim that the degree of civilization of a nation and its people is measured by the degree of tolerance towards its minorities, whether they be of a racial, religious or sexual nature, has become a truism, at least in our lay democracies. Yet prejudice dies hard, look at some of the states in America where sodomy is still deemed a crime and at those banana republic dictators for whom gays are considered no better than raving dogs who should be relegated within the confines of a nuthouse. Who is crazy, I ask you?

I keep on blabbering in my thoughts, when, at the same time, I fervently yield to this man whose existence I didn't even suspect as late as two days ago, this man who was the nephew of a nazi officer, but whose magnificent gesture towards Fabio's surviving mother has touched me to the core. Am I experiencing the birth of a new love, so pure and candid that it is reaching every cell of my being?

How I desire him and how, in my heart—or is it also in my mind?—he has become all at once so indispensable!

For what I feel cannot be solely related to the novel attraction of the flesh. Could it also be compounded by the shock of my sudden realization that I have entered a homosexual relationship? A ripple of uneasiness courses through my spine. Then, as my lover burrows deeper inside of me, I whisper to his ear:

"I love you so much." There, I've said it."

Peter slows down and looks at me, eyebrows rimmed with perspiration. His gaze is one of sudden alarm. Yet, I repeat the phrase, clearly this time, stressing each syllable, so as to bar any misunderstanding, "Yes, I love you so very much."

His lips quiver. He can't bring himself to utter the words I burn for him to spell out. He's on the verge of retracting. Then, catching his breath, he says, hoarsely:

"Alexis, don't get carried away, it could be dangerous . . ."

I interrupt him and, with a sort of anticipatory rage, as if to counter fate, I grab his ass cheeks bluntly, scratch them with my nails, and force him to resume the fucking. Then, unashamedly, I shove one finger inside his hole.

"Stop this immediately, you'll make me come!" he bursts out, panting.

"This is exactly what I want you to do," I hurl back, "that you should flood my innards with your semen, so that our lives be sealed forever."

"Don't be mad," he retorts, "we mustn't play like that with destiny!"

In response, I arch my back and heave myself, then just as soon accelerate the rocking, until our two bodies reach orgasmic unison.

He comes inside my body with tremendous force, whilst I ejaculate for the second time, letting the milky fluid spread around his navel.

# CHAPTER NINE

Overexcited, moved to the core and, at once, shaken by what I sense to be a turning point in my life, I spend a feverish night peppered with colliding images, as if I were tossed around like a snowflake in the middle of a storm. Awakened at approximately two a.m. by my coming and going to the bathroom, Peter inquires about my state. He realizes something is wrong, for I waver between bouts of euphoria and depression, and he has me swallow a pill. He then utters soothing words, but refrains at the same time from deluding me with illusions.

"You must try to rest now," he then says in a firmer tone of voice, "Chase every thought out of your mind, and tomorrow we shall resume our conversation."

I acquiesce and start feeling the calming effects of the pill.

Peter didn't wake me up until ten o'clock the following day. He's wearing a khaki outfit, with latticework sandals, as if ready for a walk in the desert; he smells of 4711 eau de cologne but I notice dark rings under his eyes. My attitude must have disturbed him quite a bit. Nevertheless, he gives me a smile that wants to be reassuring and asks:

"Do I order breakfast in the room, or would you prefer us to go and have it downstairs? By the way, you did tell your wife you would go back to Ashkelon this afternoon, didn't you?"

I nod in response, then, feeling suddenly melancholic, I beckon him to come by my side. He hesitates for a split second but then gives in. I put my arms around his waist and rest my cheek against his thigh, taking in the perfume of lavender soap mixed with eau de cologne that he exudes. He remains tense and can't wait to free himself from me.

I then tell him: "Let's go downstairs and have a bite, you must be hungry, I'm sure!" and I push him gently away.

We're alone in the dining room. Breakfast is no longer being served at this late hour but, exceptionally, Peter asked the hotelier to set a table for us and the latter gracefully obliged.

My companion has a plate of cereals, mixed with muesli and dried fruit, whereas I, even though I'm longing for scrambled eggs and bacon, prepare myself a couple of sandwiches of rye bread with cream cheese, shallots and radishes. I like that sharp taste on my tongue.

Straight off, Peter asks: "Did you ever think of getting help? I mean, we all go through difficult periods in our lives at one moment or another." In the same breath, he adds, "It happened to me, and more than once too. When it started, I was advised to consult an analyst; he was a kind and empathetic man, and I really liked him, but since that first treatment didn't seem to be enough, he himself sent me to a psychiatric hospital, where I spent several months, getting full attention from a team of specialists and nurses. I couldn't stand to look at myself any more and found the company of others unbearable. So, it was the best thing for me to do."

I tell him that I did indeed consult someone in the outskirts of Tel Aviv, but that, after the fifth session, I came to the conclusion that it was a waste of time and of energy and that I got even more depressed.

He gives me a strange look—do I read pity on his face, or is it compassion?—then says: "it probably didn't click between you and that doctor, which isn't all that rare an occurrence. You have to be patient though and persist, until you do meet the right person who will understand you. I know how difficult it is under these circumstances and how one can easily lose faith, but believe me there is always a solution."

As I keep mum, he goes on, "The other night, at Rebecca's, you told me your father divided his time between Belgium and Burundi. I have a close friend in

Brussels who works at the European Union Commission. His wife went through a severe nervous breakdown— actually she tried to commit suicide—and was treated very effectively at a clinic outside the town of Waterloo. She came out of it a new person. You should see her today, so bubbly and full of activity, running left and right. Her husband can hardly keep pace with her, and he is no laggard, either, I can tell you. I used to go and visit her there and really saw the progress each time we parted. The place is located in the middle of the woods and you would think it was a resort hotel rather than a medical institution."

My gaze suddenly locks with his and I wonder why this man for whom I feel something so strong and so totally awesome, talks of shutting me behind the walls of a madhouse. I take this as some kind of treason—so, I've become a liability and he wants to get rid of me!—and my eyes become misty with tears.

"Your father will be able to see you regularly, and your wife could come and visit you from Italy every once in a while, after all, it only takes a couple of hours by plane from Milan to Brussels. Then too," he pauses, as if on the verge of retracting, "I shall also come to see you every time I visit with my friend there, for I enjoy spending time in Belgium."

Why is he making all these plans on my behalf, what am I to him, after all? The last words of his remark suddenly strike back and I feel a flush of joy spread across my face. He does care about me, why would he otherwise promise to come to the clinic? I burn to tell him again and again that it isn't a mere infatuation, that I really, truly love him, like no one else before. Then, all at once, my thoughts stray over to Serena. My head begins to reel, to reel faster and faster, like a kaleidoscope gone crazy, splashing the pitch black night that has darkened my mind, with flashes of lightning. It is as if my brain has frozen and is crackling from all sides. I then break into a cascade of sobs.

I leave Israel with a lump in my throat and with my heart split into three parts. This country is too much to bear for me, it is at once magnificent and wrenching, magnificent, because of its lovely, colorful youth, in appearance, so joyful and nonchalant, when you see them chatting and laughing in Hebrew, a biblical language that has been revived just a few decades ago and which now reunites people who have hailed from the four corners of the world, people who had so little in common, culturally or even ethnically, except the fact that they were Jews, and thus shared a millennial history of oppression and of hope, that hope which for generations was just a fantasy and spelled these words: "Next year in Jerusalem." This country fascinates me, with its myriad of existential fragments, whilst at the same time it makes me terribly giddy, for I feel in it like a speck of dust tossed about in the middle of a sandstorm. And it is amid such a tempest, when the gap between Serena and me widened, that Peter has come forth, as if the earth was gradually changing its center of gravity.

It is in this state of confusion in my feelings and allegiances that I flew back to Milan, a city so familiar to me in the past, and which suddenly looked terribly strange and foreign, even hostile, so much so, that I felt unwanted.

# CHAPTER TEN

"How serious was it?"

"They had to break into his compartment on the Milano-Brussels Express . . . tried with a sharp paper-cutter . . . married, with a child . . . just moved to Belgium . . ."

Either she did it on purpose or thought they were far enough for me not to grasp what they were saying. The boyish-looking man whom she addressed as 'doctor' turned around to glance at me with that professional detachment which conceals, among other things, fear and hesitation.

"Eclectic background . . . lived on three continents . . . seems to have a good disposition . . ."

They walked away. It was getting dark and cold, and I felt hungry.

A stout, middle-aged Flemish nurse showed me to my room. It was in the annex, on the first floor, overlooking an orchard. At the other end stood the eighteenth-century mansion turned into a rest home.

"I hope you will feel comfortable here," said the nurse, rolling her r's dramatically. As I began to sneeze she proceeded:

"Pricking stuff, isn't it? We've had the place disinfected. I'll let in some fresh air. Ready? Take a long, deep breath!"

She braced her knees and flung the window wide open. After a few chilling seconds which allowed me to appreciate her brawny calves, she pulled down the shade.

"That's it. I'm off now," she added in a matter-of-fact tone. "Ah! If you need anything, just ring the bell to call the night nurse. I've left her instructions for your medicine. Cheerio, see you tomorrow."

I heard the heavy thump of her steps and counted them as she walked down the staircase. I could still feel her presence lingering about, in an odor of warmed-over potato chips. My lungs became slowly impregnated with it until I got nauseous.

Sat on the corner or the bed. It creaked in response. Got a fright. Eyes then roamed in a cold inspection from one object to another. Desk, empty flower pot, lithograph representing a plowman at work . . . moth-eaten curtains, wash basin surmounted by a cracked mirror, solid mahogany wardrobe, desk again, ceiling, pink lampshade, desk once more. Drew left wrist close to ear, listened attentively to ticking of watch. Three knocks at the door.

"So, how is our new guest? We seldom have young folks around. It's a nice change. By the way, are you afraid of ghosts?"

She had a big bony smile and the neck of a giraffe.

"No," I caught myself answering. "Is it any business of yours?"

"The old lady who preceded you was a sleepwalker, and your next-door neighbor used to come and pay her nightly visits. He still does it sometimes. They had known each other for nine years. But don't worry, he isn't dangerous.

I leaped to my feet as if someone had suddenly set the bed afire.

"Well," I started shouting, "I'll lock myself in!"

"Calm down! I only wanted to warn you. Anyway, there are no keys here, except for the bathroom."

I stood still and stared at her for a while, until I finally consented to swallow the pills she handed me with a glass of water.

"That's better. You should undress and try to sleep. In the meantime, I'll tidy away your linen in the cupboard."

I shook my head in a stern no. She didn't insist and was about to leave the room when I stretched my arms out to her: "Nurse, please, can I take a shower?"

"Of course . . . call me Yvonne . . . . She spoke with a strong Walloon drawl (a French dialect spoken in southern Belgium) and followed me right into the bathroom. I was in a fidget. The bottle of shampoo slipped out of my hands, with the towel. Couldn't she understand? Didn't they know what privacy meant in this place? Apparently not, for I had to strip naked in front of her, let her rub my back—where was my mother's gentle touch?—and dry me up as if I were a bundle of carrots.

"That's a good boy!" She made me blush to the point that I became obsessed with one thought: my body. Body and shame. Not the fears that had brought me here, not the austere walls of my new prison, not even the whining of a moribund patient upstairs seemed to bother me that night.

The bell chimes. We are summoned to the refectory: a wainscoted, creaking dining-room on the ground floor of the mansion. Just ten of us around the table. Presiding at each end, respectively: Mademoiselle Helene, a gentle forty-ish brunette, and Madame Liliane, her assistant, younger, lean, platinum blonde, more talkative. They seem to get on fairly well. Very seldom hear them argue. Everybody seated except for the wind-broken Monsieur Lazarus and Mademoiselle Helene who's helping him to get into his chair. At each meal, the same ritual. Average age among the inmates: seventy-five. 'Gagagenarian' atmosphere.

No one crosses him/herself. Religion doesn't seem to be a matter of concern here. Perhaps they are prudish about it. It is quite disturbing to remind God of one's existence when skirting death becomes one's major pastime.

A gust of steamed food sweeps through the refectory as Leila pushes open the kitchen door, carrying a piteously huge tray. Roar of applause, initiated by Mademoiselle Helene, who pays the bashful servant a generous compliment: "It'll be a treat, I can assure you, and a pleasant surprise for those of you who've never tasted real Algerian couscous!"

Toothless Monsieur Lazarus bursts into a fit of laughter. He almost swallows half of his napkin, chokes and sputters in his plate. Madame Liliane rushes over to the old man, pats him vigorously on the back until he is ready to drink some water.

I can hear Mr. Dupont gnash his teeth, in his own peculiar manner. Lofty and cynical, he suffers from asthma, doesn't talk much, but when it happens, no interruption is tolerated. He has two ways of approaching people. He either darts a hawkish eye upon you—which means that you are interesting enough, although not necessarily sympathetic—or, he stares fixedly at his own image, reflected and multiplied in the cutlery, as if he were all by himself.

Someone is whispering to my left . . . the ever-moaning and grumbling Countess—Austro-Hungarian, with some Russian blood, if I'm not mistaken. She's an alcoholic. Her wrinkled cheeks droop like those of an exhausted chubby cocker spaniel:

"Hate that North African stuff! Heaven knows what she's put in the soup. Ha, soup! Vegetable porridge, yes! And those red peas over there; hot enough to pop your eyes out!"

Half-bent over his plate, Monsieur Lazarus falls asleep, munching a piece of boiled carrot.

Sudden bellowing of an animal in a slaughter house. The poor old man tries to clear his throat, pokes the monumental lady at his right in the ribs; he savagely rubs his Adam's apple with the other hand. A spoon lands in the plate of one of the inmates. Floundering in his chair, eyes wide open, tongue out, Monsieur Lazarus literally capsizes, head down.

Both Mademoiselle Helene and her assistant get hold of him and drag the now unconscious mass out of the room. Silence for a while. Not a sign of surprise, not a wink. Monsieur Dupont lifts an eyebrow of contempt. The monumental lady keeps staring—glassy, unperturbed expression of someone who is above such petty physical considerations. Leila's face has turned livid:

"Anyone for some more couscous" she probes in a faint voice.

Her hand trembles as she is ladling out the soup. The Countess glares at Mr. Dupont and mutters:

"How can you even hope to get cured with such pigs around you?" Her lips are rimmed with saliva. Mr. Dupont shrugs it off, then ignores her altogether.

Once the meal is over, most of the inmates retire to the adjoining salon, waiting for their cup of coffee.

The Countess cackles on, apparently indifferent to the fact that the monumental lady opposite her is not listening. In a nervy gesture, Mr. Dupont switches on the radio full blast, then lowers it, but not until the Countess has shut up. An educated man, conscious of his superiority, he imposes the choice of his programs on the others. He always listens to the BBC's one o'clock news, monopolizing it, for no one else here understands English. Eventually, he lets them enjoy the boring 'Music-upon-request' programme. After gulping his tepid beverage, he stands up, moves to the door and bids a vague goodbye.

The Countess, in want of companionship, turns to me:

"Dreary place for a youngster like you, isn't it? I'm a grandmother, you know. You wouldn't think so, but I am. They've abandoned me, the rascals! Too much of a nuisance at home. That's why they sent me here. I'd rather be buried in the Pyramids than with these morganatic bums. They look like mummies anyway."

Ten days of insulin coma therapy. Whirlwind of faces. Always the same trio: my handsome and bespectacled doctor, the fat Flemish nurse, and Yvonne, who is helping me get dressed. I am slowly awakening from that long woolly universe, teeming with shapeless forms—the so-called deep-sleep treatment.

My limbs and I behave like strangers; they seem reluctant to obey whosoever resides under that empty sound box which once contained a mind. Is it still there? If so, I don't recognize it.

A day or two later, I find myself sitting in the refectory. Total numbness. A vacuum. Then, sudden change when my eyes meet those of the girl who is waiting on us. Olive complexion, lustrous hair dotted with crystal drops; smile so sad that I wonder whether I should call it a smile. The trembling of my hands has ceased. I tentatively regain control of my senses. It hurts. All over. Wounds in the raw. As many needles as I have pores. Can't stand the sight of the people I am sharing this meal with. Is it the projection of a renewed outbreak of self-hatred? Room reeks of death. I smell it, breathe it, hear it. The perpetual wailings of Monsieur Lazarus. The hoarse, nerve-racking grunt of the Countess. Her new dentures, already black with nicotine—she had all her teeth pulled out a month ago. Mr. Dupont, who's hissing like a snake ready to strike. And the monumental lady, ever so mute, immovable; for all I know, she might have reached the hereafter a long time ago, unless she's practicing the language of the dead—sepulchral silence. I wonder if they have such a thing as an absorption center down, or up there, whichever the case may be. Do they apply a form of apartheid—soul segregation, that is? The only one to be spared my harsh judgement is Leila. Why she in particular? Except for the monumental lady, to me, Leila is the most inscrutable character around. There has never been more between us than a laconic exchange of courtesies. A hushed "How are you today?" or an impersonal "Bon appétit!" accompanied by that bleak and somewhat indomitable smile or hers. Maybe it's the sheen of her iris.

Snow flakes spraying the air. Symphony in white major. First movement. Piano, pianissimo. The trees with their arms outstretched are the soloists of this ageless orchestra. No conductor. Armonia magica. So smooth. Blood-curdling cries. Footsteps. I'm alone in this garden of Hades. I grope in the pocket of my duffle coat for a handkerchief and extract instead a pair of red sunglasses. Which I put on. *Horresco referens*—I shudder as I relate. The whole atmosphere is bleeding. The wound can't be spotted. It is omnipresent. Fresh, rich, non-coagulating blood. Beautiful and distressing! Peaceful yet staggering. Have the gods slaughtered each other, washing the earth in an ocean of plasma?

As I approach the mansion, the faces I recognize through the stained-glass window appear as unusual as purple ghosts at a secret gathering. I enter the room, leaving my spectacles on. Red glances. Hostile smiles. Altered sensations. They speak a language I understand. Fragments of conversation—perfectly intelligible—in which I decide not to partake. I feel cloistered in a protective sheath. My lips move. They utter words, yet I can't hear them any longer. I'm probably giving the right answers. The Countess-ghost has just nodded at me, while the ghost of Mr. Dupont sneers. Who is he making fun of now?

"Wipe that grin off your face!"

No reaction. Haven't I just said it? Never mind. The intention was there. Clicking noises. The other ghosts are busy eating. Eating, chewing, swallowing blood. I'm not hungry.

"Have some! It's fresh, broiled salmon."

My hands wave a gesture of refusal. Inquisitive looks. They get on my nerves. Someone orders me to take off my glasses. Who the devil does he think he is—he or she? I don't know. It continues to nag me. I get up, push back my chair and leave the refectory, yelling:

"Return to where you came from, bunch of bloody ghosts!"

9:20 pm on my fluorescent watch. It is still snowing. The night resembles a live lacework. Dapple-grey. I'm about to cross the garden, heading towards the annex, when I hear a flutter. I turn around and see Leila shaking a tablecloth on the doorstep of the kitchen. She beckons to me, whispers something I don't quite get. Disappears for a moment, then comes out dressed in a synthetic fur coat, carrying a straw bag on her left arm.

All the lights of the mansion are out except in the living room, where the only animated object is the television screen. Ghost entertainment in a ghost house.

Again she whispers: "Alexis, Alexis . . . ."

I approach her, hesitantly.

"But why did you keep those sunglasses on during lunch?"

As no answer comes, she adds: "Would you mind accompanying me to the bus station? I'm afraid to go there alone at this hour of the night."

She's right. Not a soul around. Shadows. And the thriving, intensifying lacework of the snow. Two street lamps pathetically sustaining the assault of undetectable machine guns. The frenzy of a myriad of tiny white bullets. Sudden whoosh of an empty bus—flash of neon in the darkness. Seconds later a truck wobbles its way up the opposite direction. Then again that pervasive quietness, which is neither silence nor sound. What a grim sight indeed! . . . eerie beauty. The pavement is wide enough for only one person. Cobblestones covered with slush. I walk at the edge of the road and catch hold of Leila's sleeve:

"Be careful, you can break your neck on those things!"

She smiles, her gaze flitting now here, now there, and says:

"How thoughtful of you! My husband wouldn't mind at all if something like that happened to me."

Before I realize what she means, the trolley picks her up and they vanish in the dark.

Ten weeks already. When will I get out of here? No one has a clue. Yes, the doctor. But we're not on speaking terms. Madame Liliane and Mademoiselle Helene won't talk either. They've been instructed not to. So, I barely greet them. Leila shows compassion but can't do much. As for the other inmates, I've lost all patience. That monkey business of smiling and counter smiling is weighing on my jaws. Very soon I won't be able to utter anything but platitudes. In fact, my vocabulary has shrivelled up like an accordion. The safest thing to do is to entrench myself in that annex room on the first floor, where at least I can make faces at whatever and whomever I wish. Whims, they call it.

Serena came to see me, accompanied by my father. It's the first family visit since I am here. Initially I wondered why she had to wait for my father to return from Burundi in order for her to leave Milan. Is she too cowardly to face me alone, that she needed his presence? Or am I fantasizing again?

A light rain mixed with melting snow dots the landscape. This mushy weather is the mirror of my soul. The moment I saw them, stepping together towards me, I shed a few tears and immediately tried to buck up, feeling a twinge of remorse. Apparently I have lost the measure of things, confusing genuine sentiment with self-pity.

"Alexis, my dear, you didn't tell me anything about your intention of getting a divorce."

My father's last words echo in my ears like the thud of dead wood. I can't even remember what he said before. Have I heard right? I bore into Serena's eyes, but she avoids my gaze.

"Won't you open your mouth?" I burst out in a low raging voice.

She heaves a sigh then, says, haltingly:

"We . . . we couldn't go on like that . . . you were dragging me down . . . with your depression."

"But we didn't even approach the subject." I retort, dismayed.

Then, as if suddenly stung by a banderilla, I shout, "How foul of you, to await the return of my father to make this kind of announcement, and I'm the last one to know! Everything went so smoothly between us these last seven years. Have you forgotten? We were even considered by friends and family as the 'ideal couple', or you don't remember that either. You didn't seem unhappy at all, or was it all fake?" I lament then, picking up steam again, I growl, "Will you look at me, damn it!"

"It is true," so she does admit it, "we were happy together, but things have changed these last months, taking an ugly turn, and we began to disconnect . . ."

Calling my father to witness, I snap back, with growing fury:

"She erases the seven fat years with a stroke and can't bear the slightest hitch. So much said for loyalty! She never really loved me, this is what I'm discovering."

My nerves are so much on edge that I begin to tremble like an epileptic at the start of a fit.

"Calm down, Alexis, dear. Do you want me to call the doctor?" my father asks, in a panic.

"I don't need a doctor for this!" I retort, "So that he may trouble me even further, asking more stupid questions? No, you both better get out of here, I've heard enough."

My poor father lowers his gaze and I notice the sadness knitting his brows. He motions Serena towards the door.

I don't make a gesture to greet them, even though I'm quite aware that my father has nothing to do with this and that he doesn't deserve such harshness from me. But right now, my heart remains deaf.

The hours go by and my head is streaked with thunderous lightning, whereas the surrounding atmosphere has cleared and the rays of a frosty sun, resembling a giant fossilized egg yolk, lick the crest of the trees. The nightmare persists even during daylight, to the point where I don't know when it hurts most, while I'm awake or while I'm about to fall asleep, gliding into that danger-filled limbo induced by the heavy drugs those damn specialists force me to swallow.

On my desk lies a notepad, with a pencil next to it, and all I manage to write on the first leaf is this: my age multiplied by 0 equals 0. I then scribble away, filling page after page, diligently then obsessively, with letters and signs, mostly round signs, but also geometric signs, reminding me of the exercises we were given in first grade during spelling class.

What does that number (my age), multiplied by zero, mean? When I first wrote it, I thought it translated the will to commit suicide, but in hindsight, I believe that there still was a faint spark of hope nestled in the recesses of my soul, for isn't the zero figure also equivalent to the *tabula rasa*, that is the desire to erase all memory and start everything anew, on so-called virgin ground? Though the prospect of becoming amnesic might appear terrifying, it is like living some kind of reincarnation. Don't you have to die first before you resurrect?

The wound inflicted by the knowledge of my upcoming divorce, compounded by the professional void created when I decided to hand over my resignation at KBI, can only aggravate my sense of loss. It always amazes me how much suffering a human being can take, and how, like a virus, he becomes ever more resilient as new layers of suffering are added to the former ones, which defies and puts to the test the phrase 'I can't bear it anymore'.

It is in this state of limbo, feeling lower than ever, that three days after the visit of my father and Serena, Peter reappears. I honestly thought he'd forgotten about me, that the promise he made in Israel wasn't serious, even though he was the one to recommend this place. And, for a while I was angry at myself for having listened to him.

I get a slight shock seeing him with that red scarf tied around his neck and the thick worsted pants he wears; he looked somewhat younger when we first met, that was probably because of his shorts and his healthy buttercup tan.

He is tactful enough not to ask how I am. Did he expect to see me so drawn, so lost and haggard? In any case nothing transpires from his attitude and he behaves as if we had just parted the other day. No sooner do I introduce him to my room than he hands me a parcel wrapped in silk paper and tied with a navy blue ribbon.

"If I remember correctly, you did tell me that you enjoyed reading in Spanish, so I thought this might please you."

I look dazed, almost expressionless, but he goes on in a buoyant tone, as if he hasn't noticed:

"Well, what are you waiting for, open it!"

I comply and utter a cry of wonder when I discover its contents: a boxed set of books, the collected works of Federico Garcia Lorca, presented in the prestigious leather-bound Aguilar edition.

"My God, this is sheer folly!" I exclaim. "You must have paid a fortune for this."

"Tut tut!" he says jovially, "There is one condition however, that when you get out of here, which is quite soon, as I understand it, you give me a detailed report on the oeuvre of this major author, for you will realize what a complete artist he was, whether as a poet, as a writer—he also penned a number of important plays—as an illustrator and as a performer."

It is the first time, since being committed to this institution, that someone broaches a subject other than that of a medical nature or of its collateral effects— the gossip I hear in the living-room, the whims and eccentricities of some of the patients, mixed with the constant wheezing and complaints, as well as the other countless unpleasant occurrences, have pushed me deep into the doldrums, convincing me that this deadly atmosphere would be perpetuated for a long time to come, even when I will no longer be here, a prospect almost impossible to envision in my present state.

My eyes sting, my tongue is parched, then without any forewarning, I burst into a cascade of sobs. The portrait of my beloved Astrid unfurls in my head, as in a movie sequence, at the speed of 24 images per second, and I can't bear her absence anymore.

When I learned that my father would come, I had the intention of evoking her memory—it was such a burning need—but the moment I saw that he was accompanied by Serena, I dropped the idea, especially after the announcement of my divorce, Astrid couldn't possibly enter this picture. It was as if they had connived to keep her constricted behind the walls of my childhood memories. Yet, like a boomerang effect, I miss Africa terribly, the smell of the earth, the laterite cracking in the heat of the dry season, the sudden breeze of relief that bores deep into your lungs when the first rains pelt down with the fury of a thousand eagles, the potent odor of sweat of my African brothers, the mouth-watering chicken *mwambe*, as it simmers in palm oil, amid red beans, *pili pili*, sour spinach, hibiscus leaves and sweet potatoes, or the whiff of grilled corn, tickling your nostrils. I want my childhood back, I crave for it, with all the nerves and sinews of my body, I need to feel my mother's warm breath, her cheek resting against mine.

Peter takes my hand and presses it tightly, he half opens his mouth but ultimately remains silent.

Then, recomposing myself, I mutter:

"I have to run away from here, these people are like the living-dead of the horror movies, they will drive me completely crazy."

I notice a wrinkle of sadness on my visitor's face, there is also unconcealed compassion. He would like to embrace me, but keeps a certain distance. He doesn't want me to misinterpret a gesture that could add to my already great confusion, which I understand. When he sees that I have calmed down, he probes:

"Wouldn't you like me to speak to your doctor or to the head nurse? I honestly think the staff here is very professional and that they take your case seriously." Then, without, transition, he adds, "How about if I came to visit you every weekend from now on? Would that please you?" His last proposition fills my heart with such glee that I have to refrain myself from jumping on my two feet, lest he thinks that I've really become mad.

In a controlled, husky voice, I say:

"You would come all the way from Germany every weekend? That's too much of a sacrifice, I can't accept it."

This time he answers forthrightly, without a trace of hesitation:

"Don't worry about that. I want to see you regularly from now on, and we shall discuss your future together. We are friends, aren't we? To reassure you, that train trip takes less than three hours, during which I can work or read a good book. After all, I also need to rest my mind every once and a while."

What does this guy find in me to show such generosity of feelings, when all he has seen of my personality is the darkest and least attractive side? Isn't he projecting the childhood love he had for Fabio, the little Jewish pal his nazi uncle had abused, and who disappeared together with the countless victims of Hitler? Something tells me, and I can't pinpoint what, that it wasn't a coincidence if we both met in Israel. Is it because I am of mixed blood, half black, half Italian, the son of a Catholic mother and of a Jewish father? Some of this must fascinate him, for I do represent a symbol, that of the oppressed, whether it started with the Hebrew folk enslaved in Ancient Egypt, or the Blacks wrenched from their land by both the Arab merchants and the European colonialists. But if that's the case, he then pities me.

Did I speak out this last thought, that he should respond with a trembling voice and hawkish eyes, ready to jump at my throat?

"Who the hell do you suppose I am?" he blurts out. "Yes, you are going through a difficult period in your life, but I won't allow you to doubt my sincerity. If you prefer that we don't see each other anymore, I shan't bother you again."

A shudder courses through my spine and paralyzes me. I realize that I have gone too far, at the risk of breaking the only friendship I now have in this world, even though I still don't quite grasp all of its elements, for he is genuinely offended.

"Forgive me, Peter," I whisper, then raising my voice, I say, "It has nothing to do with you, I have lost all faith in myself, and I no longer trust anybody around me. But you are an exception. So, yes, please come back to see me. I shall await your visit eagerly. Do forgive me, I beg you!"

His temples glow with perspiration and the shadow of a smile brushes through his lips, a wounded smile.

I choose not to mention the news that hurts me so much, the divorce which I had not foreseen, for something tells me if do, it could taint our relationship. I shall have to bear that stone in my chest, without any crutches. He might otherwise think that I only attract bad luck, and part of what I said is true, I don't want him to pity me.

How difficult it is to pick up a conversation after this last incident! I keep quiet, resting the palm of my hand on one of the two volumes of Garcia Lorca's collected works, stroking the leather cover and feeling its fine grain, as though it were the nape of a young fawn. I then open the book randomly and start reading aloud verses from *Poems in New York*.

This improvised performance has the advantage of easing the atmosphere, all the while clearing up the mist in which my mind seems to be permanently shrouded, even if my gestures remain somewhat clumsy. At the same time a sense of peace invades me—this hasn't happened since the start of my breakdown. It then is on such a note that we part. Peter reiterates his promise and we embrace tenderly—nothing sexual is intended, from either side, and it's just as well, for I couldn't have stood it to find myself alone again after having made love to him.

My last evening in the rest home. I've gotten accustomed to these crinkled, indifferent, cadaverous grins. Even developed a sort of attachment to them. They're all here in the television room. Except for Monsieur Lazarus. He supposedly left with a relative . . . Gone to the country, somewhere near the coast. He's disappeared without saying goodbye. No one has ever commented on his departure, as if it were an accepted thing to vanish like that, overnight. A likeable old chap he was. Obviously, he won't return. Death doesn't bother to leave greeting cards behind, at least not here.

I give the place a cursory inspection and, with a boldness which only the spirit affords, I pry into the mind of each inmate. What right do you have? It's like wiretapping, or just about. But I can't resist the temptation. They've told me so little about themselves. It's my way of showing . . . concern. If only for the silence we've shared. I don't want to leave the party like a scoundrel. They taught me self-restraint, made me conscious of my mortality.

What is Mr. Dupont brooding over again? He's so straight and stiff in his chair. Never sits on the couch. Oh, no! That's for the 'slack buttocks' of the monumental lady. She's sneezing, poor creature.

("Poor, my foot! If you don't stop this act, I'll gag you. It wouldn't make a difference anyway, you dumb fish! Go on . . . how I'd like to see you crawl in the middle of the desert . . . and stuff two corks in those alligator nostrils of yours!")

Their eyes finally meet. His threatening, hers glowering:

("You're wasting your energy, nervous brat! I know why you're so mad at me. You have no clue as to whether I hate you or simply despise you. Keep guessing.")

Weary of her 'eternal absence,' he clears his throat and turns on the television. It howls. He is doing it on purpose. To test the audience's reaction:

("Decibels, decibels, until they pierce your eardrums and pound your sclerotic brains.")

The Countess rubs her forehead in protest, then reels as if to grab something. Tries to get up but wobbles and falls back in a grunt:

("Drunk again, hey! You clod! You wet blanket!")

Has Mr. Dupont got the message? Certainly, and that is why he plays with the knob. Lowering, increasing the volume, lowering it again:

("Blue-blooded goose. You've been to America so many times, eh. Why the hell didn't you stay there? A real pity you missed the Titanic—I would have loved to see you jump into the ocean, wheedled by some cute iceberg.")

The monumental lady lends her usual deaf ear . . . and dead eye. As soon as Mademoiselle Helene enters the room, everybody puts on a demure look. The television announcer speaks in a soft, mellifluous tone, while Mr. Dupont glances through the window, missing nothing of what goes on inside. It is night now and the window makes a perfect mirror. The Countess, a filter cigarette hanging on her lower lip, fumbles with the table lighter in front of her, striking it nervously. She strikes and strikes, obtaining only jeering sparks. Swears, then hurls it off. Mademoiselle Helene picks it up and with a firm movement of her thumb, gives her a light. The Countess grumbles an irritated "thank you," puffs and coughs, continues to puff. Gets into a spattering fit and crushes the long butt in an ashtray.

All quietens down with the appearance of Leila, followed by Madame Liliane. Coffee and tea are served. The Algerian girl does it with great skill, pouring each his habitual dose. She knows exactly who takes milk and who doesn't. There have never been any complaints about Leila. Except in the very beginning, when an old, bigoted lady almost panicked at her sight: "What, an Arab? God forbid that the Moors invade us again. They've wreaked enough havoc in Spain for centuries."

I'd like her to stay a little longer while all eyes are fastened upon the screen. But she gives me a wink, letting me understand that she isn't yet through with her work. She expects me to join her afterwards in the kitchen. I probably won't see her again. A sort of premature nostalgia settles in my chest. I shall miss this unearthly place where the trivial also has its importance.

Since Peter's visit, Garcia Lorca has accompanied me every moment of the day—I even wonder whether he doesn't pop up secretly in my dreams—he has become my life buoy. To the point where he follows me, not as my shadow, but rather as my alter ego, and it is a bit frightening, for he becomes addictive and it now appears that I can't do without him.

I have read the entirety of both volumes in the space of three days . . . and three nights: the plays, the essays, the poems, all the while admiring his drawings, with the intensity of a Benedictine monk reciting his prayers. I went back several times to the *canciones*, and to that magnificent *romancero gitano*, which explodes like a bouquet of flowers painted by Van Gogh, and I savor each word, each syllable, as if my own breath depended on it, and I articulate them, slowly, religiously, until I hear their echo reverberating inside my arteries. Indeed, this osmotic fusion frightens me and I ask myself how I could possibly face the outside world. By tying Garcia Lorca's books to my neck with a silver chain? Isn't art the consecration of utopia?

# CHAPTER ELEVEN

My return to civilian life was quite painful, not only because I got used to the surreal, mortifying atmosphere of the 'mansion'—strange as it may appear, it became my cocoon—but because in some way, I established a human, if imperfect, relationship with my analyst. He probably believed that, confronted with these elderly people who were spending the last stretch of their existence there, I would react violently and become conscious of the fact that we did not belong to the same world, for they were coming out of it whilst, as bruised as I felt, I still enjoyed the benefits of youth. Above all, I would have to rebuild myself completely, emotionally and otherwise. When I resigned from KBI, giving up an interesting and well-paid job, did I realize that I was going to change the direction of my professional life, and embrace a new career? And what would the alternative be? Something I hadn't even considered! Then came the brutal announcement of my divorce, like a boulder falling on one's house. And finally, there was the advice of my 'soul' doctor, that I should cut the umbilical chord with my past.

"You are obsessed with the memory of your mother and of Africa," he insisted, "almost as if you wanted to replay that period, when you know full well that it is harmful to you and that, as you yourself are aware, the place of your birth has drastically changed, and not at all as you would wish it to be."

I felt that something in his theory didn't quite work for me. Maybe he was right about my African nostalgia, but no way would I forget or put away the tender years I spent with my beloved Astrid, that would have meant burying her a second time. Reminiscing those moments that belong uniquely to a mother, and thinking of her when I felt sad, could only bring solace.

The worst, when you lose touch with reality is that, if, during your periods of lucidity, you realize that the person in front of you is wrong, the more so if he happens to be your analyst, you have little if any means of countering his arguments, inasmuch as he considers you ill, that is, in a condition of intellectual inferiority, which, of course, only makes you feel even more depressed.

Even if my father and I have never been very close, I must admit that he has been particularly understanding and solicitous with me in these very trying times. He has offered to share his apartment in Brussels and stay there for as long as I need, i.e., until I find my bearings—he will soon be departing for Burundi to take care of his business there. I don't have the courage to go back to my home in Milan—must I consider it my home any more, now that I'm getting separated, and that I shall have to find a new lodging? Father has accepted to relay my news to Serena, acting as our go-between, asking her to be patient, since I don't have the heart to speak to her directly. How long can I wait before I confront her again? And how will I react towards that person, my wife, who's become a stranger to me? It is so disturbing to suddenly realize you have nothing to say to the woman with whom you have shared the better part of seven years of your adult life. The feeling is excruciating, inasmuch as a gap has now settled between the mind and the flesh, getting wider each minute that passes, the more so since I have the impression that my body has not adjusted to the situation: it continues to smell her perfume, to crave her body. I probably am repeating myself, but I cannot conceive sex without love. This is the reason why—and it has nothing to do with being prude or with a sense of morality—I could never go to see prostitutes, in spite of the incitation of my college mates. This was confirmed most passionately when Peter and I made love in the room of his Tel Aviv hotel, though I felt the gap between my genuine sentiments towards him and his hesitancy. I have probably remained unabashedly candid if not naive, and maybe with time, if I ever get back on my two feet again, will I be able to put things in perspective, without becoming a cynic. But can one change one's nature, especially when confronted with a personal calamity?

Peter came to see me again two days before my father would fly back to Burundi. I had to control myself and put a certain distance between us, lest our relationship be distorted—it would have been unhealthy to cling to him, when I am still so wobbly. Yet he is the one who insisted that we keep in touch—let's not be hypocritical, I am a thousand times thankful for it and hoped he would take the initiative.

I made a point to introduce him to my father, telling the latter how helpful he was in Israel and how precious his friendship is under the present circumstances. Such a display of emotion on my part put him ill at ease, but my father never detected anything that might reveal the nature of our bond. On the contrary, he seemed reassured that we should see each other regularly during his absence, and that my new friend would continue to inquire about my 'progress' from Germany. How would he react if indeed he knew the truth about our relationship? I can't even begin to imagine. Might he disown me? "No, no," I reasoned myself, "stop thinking so negatively! Let time take its course." Those were Peter's words and, to alleviate my anguish, I have adopted them, for now that my father has left I suddenly feel the terrible gap that separates me from the so-called normal folk.

The simple fact of going to a grocery store and to have to choose a brand frightens me to the point that once I stand in front of the cashier I get cold sweat and begin to stammer. It is doubly wrenching, for at the Institution everything was presented to us on a silver platter, so to speak, and if we should go wayward there was always a member of the medical staff to intervene and 'save' us.

This environment which was once so familiar to me because I would come to Belgium, light-hearted, as a visitor now weighs on me tremendously, for I have to learn to live here alone and get used to the every day tasks a single person faces. Mornings are the most difficult, since I have to force myself to get up at a regular hour, go to the bathroom and pick out the clothes I shall wear that day. There is, of course, nobody to check up on me or to order me about, and I could stay in bed well into the afternoon, but the mere thought of leading a life of sloth and idleness, when most people have a hard time trying to make ends meet, if they are not unemployed, makes me feel guilty.

When I brush my teeth in front of the mirror, the same question comes back every time: "What's the use of repeating this mechanical gesture, day in and day out? Who is waiting for me outside, anyway?"

If someone looks at me strangely, or at least if I imagine he does, like during that incident which I witnessed yesterday afternoon in a department store—a woman just in front of me was caught red-handed stealing clothes—gives me a cold sweat.

Every now and then I still think of committing suicide, but I have taken a solemn vow in front of both my father and Peter, swearing on Astrid's memory, that I would never try to harm myself again. That promise hangs like a millstone around my neck and I can't make a move without thinking that I'm being spied on, so haunting it has become. What irks me most is that I'm dragging along this exclusive and compact load of emotions, where neither reason nor logic have their place. And so I catch myself wishing I were as cold and cynical as Mr. Dupont, whom nothing seems to disturb.

Thank goodness I have Peter. He calls me every evening from Germany and comforts me with his kind words, for it is when the lamppost in my street lights up that the anguish starts welling in my chest. It is even worse than in the morning. It probably has to do with the luminosity to which I was used in Africa, for when night falls there, even after a terrifying cloudburst, the sky retains a translucent quality. This too explains my aversion to natural darkness when it is overcast, and to dull lights, whether on a theater stage, in movie scenes or even in some posh restaurants where a candlelight is set on your table for a touch of romanticism. It's almost instinctive, the moment the sun glides behind the horizon, it is as if an army of elves and evil spirits begin to stagger out of every nook and cranny, of every attic, pantry, wardrobe and drawer, and I hear those bone-chilling sounds that remind me of Dracula, slowly, inexorably, lifting the cover of his coffin. Whenever my eyes rest on some suspicious or murky space, I repeat to myself, as an act of exorcism, like a simpleton: "Light. Let there be light!"

# CHAPTER TWELVE

It's ages since I have felt so elated, so carefree. Peter has had the marvellous idea of inviting me to Heidelberg, where he teaches at the university—he tells me with pride that it's the oldest in the country. What a quaint and charming old town it is. I love strolling along its cobbled streets, pushing open the door of a *Konditorei* and taking in that wonderful smell of freshly baked pastry, mixed with wafts of hot chocolate, marzipan and cinnamon. Or else entering one of the countless *Bierstuben* patronized by young people, students for the most part, where the atmosphere is noisy and joyful. Strangely enough, the crowd here doesn't disturb me, whereas I would be transfixed if it had taken place in Milan. If someone happens to bump into you, getting out of a store or of a tram, he excuses himself or even asks if you haven't been hurt. And I always get the same thrill, crossing the Old Bridge over the Neckar River that leads to the hill where Goethe and the other romantic poets would admire the city in its lush green setting, dominated by the splendid thirteenth century castle, which miraculously escaped the intense ally bombing during World War II.

There is a song that starts with this line, "Ich habe mein Herz in Heidelberg verloren." But in my case the opposite is true, for it is in this historical town of the Palatinate that my heart has started to beat again with the echoes of happiness. And I certainly don't want to lose it, either because of a stupid blunder or some misplaced pride.

Peter tells me I may stay at his place for as long as I wish. He's put me in the guestroom. It's small but oh so *gemütlich*, with the bed high on its legs, its thick eiderdown, stuffed with geese feathers, its rustic furniture and its dormer window that opens onto the forest, with, at mid-level, a patch of sky, so that pending on the weather, the range of colors stretches from a deep cerulean to cotton white, with, in between, all the shades of blues and grays, skirting the perennial green of the pine trees.

I'm often on the brink of tears—this may sound maudlin, yet I can't help it—for I still am quite vulnerable. Not that I doubt the authenticity of Peter's friendship, it is my reactions I'm afraid of. I would so much like to express the love I feel for him, but I must contain myself. Something tells me it is reciprocal, but that, for my good, he doesn't want to rush things, lest the fragile balance on which I tread should be shaken. Why else would he constantly remind me that healing is a very long process and that I should arm myself with patience? And he compares my case with that of someone who has miraculously escaped from a terrible accident, suffering multiple wounds, who needs crutches before he can learn to walk again normally.

Thanks to his tactful and unfailing support, I could pick up the courage to call Serena. In Brussels I didn't have the strength to do it. She was astonishingly receptive to my fragility. "Take your time," she said, "I've got in touch with a divorce lawyer, here. You will choose one as soon as you decide to come back to Milan."

After I hung up, it took me a while before I could measure the seriousness of that conversation, for, at first, her monotone misled me—the sweetness of it—taking me back to the good old days of wine and roses, when not a cloud marred our love; deep inside, and in spite of the fact that my mind said: 'it is finished', there remained that flicker of hope which the violence of the hurricane couldn't extinguish, and which gave me the illusion that a miracle could still take place, that we could make up and start all over again as before. But as we spoke, after inquiring about my health, of my short-term plans, the harshness of reality struck me and I staggered.

It should come to me as no surprise, yet I still can't associate Serena's mellifluous tone with a subject as cruel and repulsive as divorce procedures. There's no doubt anymore, my wife has turned the page and wishes to get her freedom back. 'My wife', how odd it sounds all of a sudden, since we are no longer treading the same path. And how obsolete the whole notion of belonging suddenly appears! Does one person ever belong to another, at least, in our so-called liberated Western societies?

I believed I knew Serena well enough to anticipate her reactions, and that we were both mutually empathetic. We were so understanding of each other that our environment considered us the perfect couple, when all around us so many marriages were disintegrating and more and more couples were getting separated, for it is only recently that divorce has become legal in Italy, a country where, unlike in northern Europe, family ties remain very strong and where the word *fidanzamento* still retains its romantic accents—an engagement Italian style can last years.

How suddenly can our convictions be shattered! We have the tendency to discard certain thoughts, believing that they only concern other people.

Thank goodness Peter is back, for I am again in a state of shock. He grasps at once the cause of it all and tries to calm me down. When he sees that his soothing words have little effect, he turns around and, in a firmer tone, offers to accompany me to Milan, during my first appearance in court.

"Since it coincides with our winter break, here, I can take a week off and play the tourist, paying a leisurely visit to the Brera museum. Also, I have never been on top of the *Duomo* to admire the golden Madonnina, with all those marble statues of saints and that fantastic Gothic lacework. Of course we shall be together again as soon as you leave the Court of Justice and, since you have lived there for ten years, you shall be my personal guide and you will show me the secret sides of Milan."

I feel somewhat appeased and Peter asks me a number of questions about my life in Italy, before I met Serena. I then tell him how relieved I am that he will be next to me while I will have to face the unpleasantness of going to court and of discussing money matters and property. My father has recommended a divorce lawyer who is apparently well known in the city circles for his efficiency. He may also rejoin me, but that will depend on his business in Burundi.

A year and a half has elapsed since I left the rest home. Serena and I have gotten our divorce at last; the most important thing now is that Peter and I are together. He has waited until all the legal hurdles were behind us before he could declare his love for me, clear and loud. That happiness for which we fought so dearly—after all, it grew out of the mental morass in which I was plunged—is finally ours. And to think that I wouldn't have known any of this had I jumped off the Shalom Tower in Tel Aviv! Indeed, 'ich habe mein Herz in Heidelberg gefunden.' (I have found my heart again in Heidelberg).

# ABOUT THE AUTHOR

A bilingual author, Albert Russo writes in both English and French, his two 'mother tongues'. He is the recipient of many awards, such as The American Society of Writers Fiction Award, The British Diversity Short Story Award, several New York Poetry Forum Awards, Amelia Prose and Poetry awards and the Prix Colette, among others. He has also been nominated for the W.B. Yeats and Robert Penn Warren poetry awards. His work, which has been praised by James Baldwin, Pierre Emmanuel, Paul Willems and Edmund White, has appeared worldwide in a dozen languages. His African novels have been favorably compared to V.S. Naipaul's work, which was honored with the Nobel Prize for Literature in 2001. He is a member of the jury for the Prix Européen and sat in 1996 on the panel of the prestigious Neustadt Prize for Literature, which often leads to the Nobel Prize.

His most recent novels are, in English: ZANY, ZAPINETTE NEW YORK, MIXED BLOOD and ECLIPSE OVER LAKE TANGANYIKA, all three with Domhan Books (NY); in French: l'ANCETRE NOIRE and LA TOUR SHALOM, both with Editions Hors Commerce (Paris), and SANG MELE OU TON FILS LEOPOLD, published by Ginkgo Editeur (Paris). Last publications in English, with Xlibris (USA): THE BENEVOLENT AMERICAN IN THE HEART OF DARKNESS (the trilogy of his award-winning African novels: 'The Black Ancestor', 'Mixed Blood' and 'Eclipse over lake Tanganyika'), OH ZAPERETTA! (the hilarious series, taught at the Catholic University of Paris), and THE CROWDED WORLD OF SOLITUDE, his collected stories and poetry in two volumes; volume 1, the collected stories, won an honorable mention at the 13th Writer's Digest International Awards.

# Also by Albert Russo
in both English and French

* Eclats de malachite, novel, Editions Pierre Deméyère, Brussels, Belgium, 1971.
* La Pointe du Diable, novel, Editions Pierre Deméyère, Brussels, Belgium, 1973.
* Mosaïque Newyorkaise, novella, Editions de l'Athanor, Paris, France, 1975.
* Albert Russo, Anthology 1, fiction and poetry, Légèreté Press, USA, 1987.
* Sang Mêlé ou ton fils Léopold, novel, Editions du Griot, Paris, France, 1990.
  —France Loisirs, Paris, France, 1991.
* Le Cap des illusions, novel, Editions du Griot, Paris, France, 1991.
* Dans la nuit bleu-fauve / Futureyes, poetry, Le Nouvel Athanor, Paris, France, 1992.
* Kaleidoscope, poetry, The Plowman, Canada, 1993.
* Eclipse sur le lac Tanganyika, novel, Le Nouvel Athanor, Paris, France, 1994.
  —Element Uitgevers, Dutch edition, 1996.
* Venitian Thresholds, fiction and poetry, Bone & Flesh Publications, USA, 1995.
* Painting the Tower of Babel, poetry, New Hope International, GB, 1996.

* Zapinette Vidéo, novel, Éditions Hors Commerce, Paris, France, 1996.
* Poetry and Peanuts, poetry, Cherrybite Publications, GB, 1997.
* Zapinette Video, novel, Xlibris, USA, 1998.
* Mixed Blood, novel, Domhan Books, USA/GB, 2000.
* Eclipse over Lake Tanganyika, novel, Domhan Books, USA/GB, 2000.
* L'amant de mon père, novel, Le Nouvel Athanor, Paris, France, 2000.
  —Edizioni Libreria Croce, Italian translation by Mario Sigfrido Metalli, Rome, Italy, 2002
* Zapinette à New York, novel, Editions Hors Commerce, Paris, France, 2000.
* Zany, Zapinette New York, novel, Domhan Books, USA/GB, 2001.
* Beyond the Great Water, Vol.1, Collected stories, Domhan Books, USA/GB, 2001.
* Unmasking Hearts, Vol.2, Collected stories, Domhan Books, USA/GB, 2001.
* The Age of the Pearl, Vol.3, Collected stories, Domhan Books, USA/GB, 2001.
* Zapinette chez les Belges, Editions Hors Commerce, Paris, France, 2001.
* L'amant de mon père II: Journal romain, novel, Editions Hors Commerce, 2003.

* L'ancêtre noire, novel, Editions Hors Commerce, Paris, France, 2003.
* The Benevolent American in the Heart of Darkness, a trilogy of 3 African novels set in the former Belgian Congo and Rwanda-Urundi, Xlibris, USA, 2005.
* Oh Zaperetta! The hilarious Zapinette series, Xlibris, USA, 2005.
* The Crowded World of Solitude, Volume 1, the collected stories, Xlibris, USA, 2005.
* The Crowded World of Solitude, Volume 2, the collected poems, Xlibris, USA, 2005.
* La Tour Shalom, Editions Hors Commerce, Paris, France, 2005.
* Body glorious, photography by Albert Russo, Xlibris, USA, 2006.
* Albert Russo, a poetic biography, vol.1&2, by Eric Tessier, Xlibris, USA, 2006.
* Sardinia, photography by Albert Russo, Xlibris, USA, 2006.
* Israel at heart, photography by Albert Russo, Xlibris, USA, 2007.
* Quirks / Eclats, photography by Albert Russo, Xlibris, USA, 2007.
* RainbowNature, photography by Albert Russo, Xlibris, USA, 2007.
* Italia Nostra, photography by Albert & Alexandre Russo, Xlibris, USA, 2007.

* Pasion de España, photography by Albert Russo, Xlibris, USA, 2007.
* City of Lovers / City of Wonder—Parie la Grosse Pomme, photography by Albert Russo, Xlibris, USA, 2007.
* New York at heart, photography by Albert Russo, Xlibris, USA, 2007.
* Sang Mêlé ou ton fils Léopold, novel, Ginkgo Editeur, Paris, France, 2007.

# Collective works

* All stories, All kinds, TVR, Peninhand Press, USA, 1985.
* Who's been sleeping in my brain? bilingual English-German anthology, Suhrkamp Verlag, Germany, 1987.
* Snow Summits in the Sun, Poetry Anthology, The Cerulean press, USA, 1988.
* The Cerulean Anthology of Sci-Fi/Outer Space/ Fantasy Poetry, USA, 1999.
* Bibliophilos Poetry Anthology, USA, 2001.
* ROMAdiva, photography by Albert Russo, texts by Eric Tessier, Albert Russo, Daniel Michelson and Sébastien Doubinsky, in English, French and Italian, Xlibris, USA, 2004.
* Chinese / puzzle / chinois, photography by Albert Russo, texts by Albert Russo, Daniel Michelson,

Eric Tessier and Sébastien Doubinsky, in English and French, Xlibris, USA, 2004.

* Le tour du monde de la poésie gay (an international anthology of gay poetry), edited and partly translated into French by Albert Russo, Editions Hors Commerce, Paris, France, 2004.
* AfricaSoul, photography by Albert Russo and Elena Peters, texts by Albert Russo, Eric Tessier, Elena Peters and Jérémy Fraise, in English and French, Xlibris, USA, 2005.
* In France, photography by Albert Russo, texts by Eric Tessier, Albert Russo, Shakespeare, Victor Hugo & Co., in English and French, Xlibris, USA, 2005.
* Mexicana, photography by Albert Russo, texts by Eric Tessier, Albert Russo, in English, in French and in Spanish, Xlibris, USA, 2005.
* Sri Lanka, photography by Albert Russo, texts by Eric Tessier, Albert Russo, in English and in French, Xlibris, USA, 2006.
* Brussels Ride, photography by Albert Russo, texts by Eric Tessier, Albert Russo, in English, in French, Xlibris, USA, 2006.
* Saint Malo with love, photography by Albert Russo, texts by Eric Tessier, Albert Russo, in English, in French, Xlibris, USA, 2006.